THE MISFITS

A ROYAL CONUNDRUM

THE MISFITS

A ROYAL CONUNDRUM

BOOK ONE

Written by **LISA YEE**

Illustrated by **DAN SANTAT**

Random House 🏠 New York

Text copyright © 2024 by Lisa Yee
Jacket art and interior illustrations copyright © 2024 by Dan Santat

All rights reserved. Published in the United States by Random House Children's Books, a division of Penguin Random House LLC, New York.

Random House and the colophon are registered trademarks of Penguin Random House LLC.

Visit us on the Web! rhcbooks.com

Educators and librarians, for a variety of teaching tools, visit us at RHTeachersLibrarians.com

Library of Congress Cataloging-in-Publication Data is available upon request.
ISBN 978-1-9848-3029-6 (trade)—ISBN 978-1-9848-3030-2 (lib. bdg.)—
ISBN 978-1-9848-3032-6 (ebook)

Printed in the United States of America
10 9 8 7 6 5 4 3
First Edition

Random House Children's Books supports the First Amendment
and celebrates the right to read.

Penguin Random House LLC supports copyright. Copyright fuels creativity, encourages diverse voices, promotes free speech, and creates a vibrant culture. Thank you for buying an authorized edition of this book and for complying with copyright laws by not reproducing, scanning, or distributing any part in any form without permission. You are supporting writers and allowing Penguin Random House to publish books for every reader.

For Rob, who doesn't know that I'm a secret crime fighter. Well, okay. So now he knows.

THe MiSFiTs

A ROYAL CONUNDRUM

1.
OLD SCHOOL

Weird things had a tendency of happening to Olive Cobin Zang, but this morning was weirder than most.

First, her InstaFriends social media account had vanished entirely—never mind that she had fewer than five followers. Then, when she opened her locker to grab her books before class, all traces that Olive had ever been there had been removed, including her Meggie comics and flower power stickers. And at the school library, when Olive tried to apologize for her overdue library books, she learned that all the fines had been wiped clean.

By the time Olive reached second period, she was so deep in thought that at first she didn't notice the black cat perched on the classroom's window ledge. Unlike her classmates, who never paid any attention to her, the cat was staring right at Olive. When she finally noticed it, it seemed to wink at her before running away.

1

Olive watched the cat disappear, wishing she could run away, too. She hated school. A lot.

Turning to the front of the room, Olive heard the school's PA system crackle. Then a tinny voice said, *"Olive Cobin Zang"*—Olive tried not to panic—*"please report to Principal Gates's office immediately."*

Instantly, prying eyes were on her. She felt her face flush red. Often overlooked, Olive did not long for *this* sort of attention. As she began to gather her books, the teacher shook her head. "Leave those. You won't be needing them anymore."

Olive bolted from the classroom, her heart racing. The last time she was called out of class, a mere month earlier, she had been informed that her beloved grandmother Mimi was gone. Who would it be this time?

Upon entering the principal's office, she saw her mother seated across from Principal Gates. Olive was instantly relieved—then panicked.

"Is it Dad?" Her brown eyes began to fill with tears.

Olive's mother, Dr. Cobin Zang, arched an eyebrow and handed her a tissue. As usual, she looked perfectly polished, making her daughter feel like a "before" photo in a fashion magazine. "Hello to you, too," Dr. Cobin Zang said gently. "Your father is fine."

"Then . . . ," Olive sputtered. "Then why are you here?" It wasn't even 10:30 a.m. She paused to note that her mother's new short haircut made her look stylish and chic, two words that were never used to describe Olive.

Dr. Cobin Zang offered Principal Gates a perfunctory smile before turning back to her daughter. "I'm taking you out of school," her mother said.

Principal Gates yawned, flipped open a magazine, and stuck his nose in the pages.

Still holding the tissue, Olive asked hopefully, "For the day?"

"Yes . . . ," Dr. Cobin Zang said cautiously, "and then some." Her mother bit her lip the way she did when she suddenly remembered something Olive-related. "I meant to tell you yesterday, but I got swamped."

Now that Olive knew no one had perished, her heartbeat returned to normal. Maybe they were going on a girls' day? That's what Mimi had called it when she'd let Olive cut school so they could go to the movies or the mall. On occasion, Olive even did this on her own, though she usually ended up at the library.

Principal Gates squinted at Olive over his magazine. "You are Olive . . . ?"

When the principal couldn't remember her last name, Olive could feel herself shrinking. Not literally, of course, but in the oh-here-we-go-again-I-feel-invisible sort of way.

Olive tamped down her discomfort. Invisibility had its benefits, she was quick to remind herself. Say assassins were chasing you, or a teacher asked about cell homeostasis and you hadn't done your homework—if they couldn't see you, you were safe from embarrassment or death, which often felt like the same thing.

Still holding his magazine in one hand, Principal Gates clicked through his computer with the other. His unkempt black hair stuck up in two places, reminding Olive of the cat

4

from second period. "This is odd, but we have no record of you. Did you say you were a student here?"

Olive began to deflate like a tire with a slow leak. "I've been a student here since kindergarten." She pushed her student ID across the desk as proof.

Principal Gates examined the dented plastic card. "Per this, you're Olive Cobin Zang, age twelve?"

"She's not twelve, she's eleven," Dr. Cobin Zang said without looking up. She was now furiously tapping on her cell phone.

Olive winced. "Actually, I am twelve."

Her mother stopped mid-text and studied Olive. "When did that happen?"

"Same time as last year," Olive muttered. She eyed her mother's phone. Even though everyone at her school had a cell phone, she could never bring herself to ask her parents for one. Besides, who would she call? It wasn't as if there was ever an emergency, anyway. Olive's life was so boring.

"Well then!" Dr. Cobin Zang straightened the lapels of her gray wool suit. "We shall have a belated birthday celebration when your father and I return."

When your father and I return. How many times had Olive heard that before? She pretended to be pleased about the celebration, but she knew they'd forget. They always did. She had no doubt that her parents loved her. Still, they never hesitated to go on their endless business trips. They always brought her back a snow globe, as if this made up for leaving.

Olive tried to convince herself that a missed birthday

wasn't *that* important. After all, her grandmother Mimi had said, "I wouldn't mind skipping a few birthdays now and then!"

Suddenly Olive was hit by a discomforting thought. In her parents' eyes, maybe the thing that wasn't important . . . was her.

She was barely three months old the first time her mother and father had left her in the care of Mimi. "You were always very adaptable," her parents would say with pride. "You never cried."

It was no wonder Olive loved the *Meggie & Her Fun Family* comic books. She dreamed of uproarious family adventures by day and home-cooked meals every night. Meggie's mother and father never went on business trips. If Olive had learned to cry, would her parents have stayed home more?

Principal Gates set his magazine down. The headline— "GLORIOUS DAME GLORIA!"—blared merrily up at Olive. The cover showed an older woman with unnaturally smooth skin, wearing an overflow of snazzy jewels on her neck, ears, wrists, and fingers. But it was the small black cat brooch with glittery green eyes on Dame Gloria's gown that caught Olive's eye.

"Well!" Principal Gates declared. "Bon voyage to you, Oliver Corbin Zing!" He hoisted his mug in the air, spilling coffee all over Dame Gloria.

"Olive Cobin Zang," Olive and her mother corrected him. Both looked at each other, startled but pleased to be in sync for a change. Was this a mother-daughter bonding

6

moment? Olive wondered. Meggie and her mother had one at least every five pages.

"Where will you be going?" Principal Gates mopped up the coffee from the magazine. Dame Gloria's face was starting to wrinkle.

Dr. Cobin Zang beamed. "Olive will be attending the acclaimed Reforming Arts School near San Francisco," she announced proudly.

Principal Gates looked stunned. "The prison?!"

Olive tried to speak, but no sound came out.

"*Former* prison," Dr. Cobin Zang said firmly. "They haven't had a prisoner there for years."

2.

RASH?

"Prison?" Olive asked her mother as they got in the car. Her throat was suddenly dry. "I'm going to prison?" she finally managed to ask.

Was Olive being punished because she repeatedly freed the neighbor's rabbits from their overcrowded pen? Or maybe it was because she broke into that abandoned haunted cottage to try to meet a ghost. . . .

All right, *maybe* Olive had bent a few rules over the years. Invisibility had its benefits, and she wasn't about to let them go to waste. Yet she was *sure* she had never gotten caught.

Dr. Cobin Zang's car backed out of the school parking lot, leaving skid marks in its wake. "You're not going to prison," she said brightly. "You're going to RASCH. You'll love it!"

"Rash?" Last year, Olive had gotten a rash from her class nature field trip. One of the popular girls, Kelsey Lawrence, had pointed at a patch of poison ivy and said, "If you want to be my friend, touch that plant."

The horrible itch lasted days longer than Olive's friendship with Kelsey, who later declared, "I don't hang around with misfits."

"R-A-S-C-H, RASCH," her mother enunciated, though to Olive it sounded exactly the same as "rash." "It's the original Reforming Arts School, a top-tier boarding academy. Very prestigious, on its own quaint little island. You could learn how to swim!"

Olive felt herself gasping for air as fear washed over her. They both knew what had happened the last time she tried to swim, or had her mother forgotten that, too? She had seemed scattered lately.

"So, I'm being shipped off to a boarding school?" Olive could hear the distress in her own voice. Not that she was sad to leave her school, where she had never fit in, anyway. But at least there she knew what to expect—the boring classes, the bullies, the subpar cafeteria lunches. All Olive knew about boarding schools involved wizards, flying brooms, and house elves, but those were only in books. "Why—?" she started to ask.

Dr. Cobin Zang held up a finger and angled her head toward the radio. The newscaster was reporting: *Jaguar Gems has been robbed, making this the fifth ultra-expensive jewelry store targeted in as many days. And now here's the countdown to this week's Top Ten Greatest Hits. . . ."*

Dr. Cobin Zang turned down the radio and swerved into the fast lane. "Olive, unforeseen circumstances are dictating this. Your father and I have an extended business trip. This one may be for months, and there's no one to take care of you, and you're still only eleven—er, twelve, and . . ."

The more the excuses piled on, the more Olive missed her grandmother. Mimi had always been on call to stay with Olive when her parents were away. She even kept a packed suitcase by her door for those emergency trips Olive's parents were sometimes sent on.

Olive loved spending time with Mimi. Whenever they were together, her grandmother would stuff Olive with Chinese delights like take-out mapo tofu and slippery chow fun noodles. For dessert, they often split a container of peppermint ice cream.

Tragically, she didn't even have a chance to say a final goodbye to Mimi. No one would even tell Olive what had happened. "She's no longer with us" was all her mother would say, tearfully.

Olive was expected to zigzag through grief on her own. She had long suspected that her parents withheld information in a misguided attempt to shelter her. But from what— the truth? How much more painful could that be?

In the Meggie comic books, her fun family discussed everything, including Meggie needing braces and Meggie's mom losing her job—but getting a better one. They had no secrets.

Now, with Mimi gone, Olive felt empty and lost. To make matters even worse, she was being banished to a boarding school.

". . . and so," her mother continued as they pulled up to their unremarkable two-story house, "we decided that RASCH would be the best place for you!" In a failed attempt to sound cheerful, Dr. Cobin Zang's voice hit an unnaturally high pitch, like she was about to break into song. "That sound good to you?"

"Not at all," Olive said glumly. But by then her mother was already out of the car. Olive unbuckled her seat belt and dragged herself inside.

When she got to her room, her mother was standing by the window, grinning. She stepped aside and pointed. "I got us matching suitcases!" Dr. Cobin Zang sang with the enthusiasm of the lady in the detergent commercial who had just removed the stubborn stains from her husband's shirt. "Look, Olive! Orange, your favorite color!"

"Orange is *your* favorite color," she reminded her mother. Olive's room was painted purple, with purple bookshelves weighed down by dozens of snow globes, plus a purple comforter Mimi had helped Olive pick.

"Hurry and pack," Dr. Cobin Zang instructed. "I'll do the same. We have to get on the road soon."

When did her mother even buy the suitcases? Didn't she say she'd just learned about the business trip? Eyeing the orange suitcase, Olive slumped into her desk chair and opened her laptop. She typed "RASCH" in the search bar.

Instead of a school website, the first thing that popped up was an ad: "FOGGY ISLAND TOUR! EXPERT TOUR GUIDES! FAMILY DISCOUNTS!"

Olive blinked and then rubbed her eyes. She was going to school at a tourist attraction?

Relentlessly upbeat music accompanied images of a huge castle. "Foggy Manor has been a monastery, a yoga retreat, and a prison," a woman intoned. "Over a hundred years ago, Remy Triste bought Foggy Island off the San Francisco coast for his bride and began building the grandest mansion in America. However, she perished under mysterious circumstances before it was completed, and Remy died of a broken heart. . . ."

Mimi would have loved this, Olive thought. Her grandmother relished a good mystery, though it was a little odd that the school wasn't mentioned at all.

"Are you almost done packing?" Dr. Cobin Zang stuck her head into Olive's room. "We don't want to be late!"

Olive shut down her computer. She scribbled in her diary, held it briefly to her chest, and tossed it into the suitcase along with her clothes and *Meggie & Her Fun Family* comics. With a heavy sigh, Olive took one last look around her room, taking in her unmade bed, the vintage poster of the famous Flying Wallendas acrobat family, and the overabundance of snow globes. Could you feel homesick when you were still at home?

Olive shut the door and then trudged back to the car.

Her mother seemed lost in thought, which was often the case before a business trip. Olive knew enough not to bother her when she got this way. Anyway, the four-hour drive (three if Dr. Cobin Zang sped) allowed Olive time to overthink about what lay before her.

Her parents' business trips had grown longer as she'd gotten older. They were gone three months for their last trip, and her mother couldn't even say when they'd be returning this time. Olive kept making the window go up and down until her mother asked her to stop. At least a new school meant she could start over, right? Maybe she'd even make a friend at RASCH.

The hum of the car's engine was hypnotic, and Olive stared at the blur of trees rushing past. *"This time, a trio of supermodels were targeted,"* the radio DJ was saying. *"Rumors are swirling that there's a criminal mastermind on the loose who's overly fond of expensive baubles. . . ."*

3.
RASCH

Olive's mother gently shook her awake. "We've arrived!" She motioned out the car window to the dark water of the San Francisco Bay.

Olive stretched her arms and stared at the blob in the ocean. A whale? An iceberg? It was hard to see through the fog.

"Things will clear up eventually," her mother promised. They climbed out of the car, and Dr. Cobin Zang waved to something in the distance. "Look! The welcome committee is waiting for you."

Through the fog, Olive could barely see the small figure standing beside a big yellow school bus.

Without warning, Dr. Cobin Zang pulled her into an uncharacteristic hug. Suddenly wide awake, Olive stiffened before allowing herself to melt into her mother. She held tight and thought about Mimi while trying to ignore the painful twinge in her chest.

"I love you," Olive whispered. She had forgotten to tell her grandmother this the last time they said goodbye, and she wasn't going to make the same mistake twice.

"Oh, Olive, honey, I love you, too." Dr. Cobin Zang's eyes began to well up. Tears? Allergies? A little of both, perhaps? For a moment, her mother looked like she wanted to tell Olive something, but instead she cleared her throat. "Your father and I will see you soon! Olive, have a wonderful time at RASCH. It may surprise you." Then she waved to the figure in the distance, got back in the car, and sped off without missing another beat.

Olive was watching her mother's car disappear into the fog when a booming voice thundered: "Olive Cobin Zang? Girl, show yourself!"

Olive jumped. She whipped her head around but couldn't see anything.

"Darn fog." The booming voice sounded resigned. "It's like pea soup, only without the flavor."

Emerging from the haze, a tiny woman strode purposefully toward her. She was wearing a yellow rain slicker, red rubber boots, and goggles.

"You must be Olive. I'm Yashika Banerjee, but everyone calls me Yash." She extended her hand and grabbed Olive's in a surprisingly strong grip. "I'm here to ferry you to RASCH." Before Olive could respond, the woman abruptly spun around and marched back into the fog. "Let's go. Don't dawdle!"

Olive swallowed her sadness. Dragging her suitcase, she struggled to stay in step with Yash, who by now had climbed into the big school bus. Olive had barely made it inside when the vehicle lurched and headed straight toward the ocean.

"Watch out!" Olive screamed as they plunged into the water.

"Amphibious vehicle," Yash explained dryly. The bus was now bouncing up and down as if in cahoots with the waves. "Meet BoBu—it's short for 'boat bus.' It can travel on both land and sea. Any other questions?"

In fact, Olive had a boatload of questions, but they all evaporated when the sun cracked through the clouds to reveal a stunning San Francisco Bay. The water glistened, seagulls swooped and cawed, and the Golden Gate Bridge stood majestically as a backdrop. It was as lovely as a screen saver and reminded Olive of the postcards her parents sometimes sent.

Yash pointed toward a small island with what looked like a castle perched on it. "Foggy Manor," she said lovingly.

Olive's eyes widened as she recognized the massive stone structure from the video. She wasn't sure if the mansion was ugly or beautiful or both. Tall turrets of irregular heights pierced the sky. Stained-glass windows shone like gems,

and unattractive gargoyles jutted out from the walls. A narrow moat wrapped around the building like a ribbon.

It was like stepping onto a movie set. Olive felt a tranquil sense of awe and wonder and, for a brief moment, a sense of belonging, even though she had never been here before.

Yash pulled up to a dock next to the water, and BoBu motored onto it as smoothly as if they'd been on land all along. As the bus rumbled to a stop, Olive was embarrassed to have been nervous when BoBu first plunged into the ocean. "The unexpected can be exhilarating," Mimi once said. "Keep an open mind and give things a chance before judging too quickly."

Yash yanked hard on a metal lever and the door swung open. "Well, come on. What are you waiting for? Sunny's expecting you!"

Olive stood up and followed Yash off the bus. As her suitcase bumped along the cobblestone walkway leading

up the hill toward Foggy Manor, she asked, "Where are the other students?"

Yash snapped her fingers. As if on cue, a loud bell rang. Kids began spilling out of Foggy Manor in tight groups, gabbing away. Their colorful clothes looked like costumes with an array of clashing patterns and styles. *Artsy-fartsy,* Olive thought approvingly, momentarily forgetting her uncertainty. "Artsy-fartsy" was lobbed around as an insult at her old school, but here it seemed to be the norm. Several students smiled at Olive despite not even knowing her, and Olive found herself smiling back.

Rising above them was a woman in a billowing caftan of green and gold, wearing a crown of daisies and a thick brown braid that went halfway down her back. She wafted in their direction, bringing with her the scent of pomegranate and patchouli that Mimi was so fond of.

"Olive!" she exclaimed in a rich voice. As she neared, it quickly became apparent that she was as tall as Yash was short. "I'm Sunny O'Moa. I'm sure your parents have told you about me. We went to school together and were all on the fencing team!"

Olive hadn't known her parents fenced, and she certainly had never heard of Sunny O'Moa. Uncertain whether to tell the truth or lie, Olive decided on something in between. "You're Sunny!" she said.

"Indeed!" A rosy blush spread across her pale cheeks. "As dean, I'd like to formally welcome you to RASCH—Oof! Oof! Oof!"

When Olive looked unsure, Sunny nodded to Yash, who managed an unenthusiastic "Oof."

"Now you say it, Olive." Sunny smiled in anticipation.

". . . Oof?"

"Oof! Oof! Oof!" Sunny's voice carried in the wind. She grinned. "It's our official RASCH greeting! You'll get the hang of it."

This was it. This was her moment to ask. Olive swallowed. "Pardon me . . ." Olive was capable of being exceedingly polite when necessary. "But . . . what kind of school *is* RASCH?"

When Sunny beamed at her, Olive felt warm inside. Maybe this place wouldn't be so bad after all. "Excellent question! Bravo, Olive!" She swept a hand toward the manor and the kaleidoscope of students who occupied the lawn. "Our revolutionary Reforming Arts School was founded decades ago as an experiment in schooling juvenile offenders. Today, we are a boarding school for the artistically adventurous!"

Any hope Olive had allowed herself was tossed aside when she heard the words "juvenile offenders." Did Sunny think she was a juvenile offender? *Was* she a juvenile offender? Was relocating lawn gnomes considered a crime? Was RASCH still a prison of sorts?

Numbly, Olive wondered if she would perish here. Was there a doctor on call? She was starting to get a stomachache.

"Do you have any questions?" Sunny asked brightly.

Olive shook her head. "No, everything's good," she said softly, then forced a smile. "Oof?"

4.
FOGGY MANOR

Sunny's bracelets jangled like the melodious wind chimes that circled Mimi's circus tent. "As you can see, the mansion is an architectural masterpiece," she noted proudly. "Though this island is made entirely of rock, the original owner of Foggy Manor, Remy Triste, imported rich soil from Italy; hence the lush gardens!"

The breathtaking landscape was dotted with students—on the lawns, in the trees, atop the boulders overlooking the ocean. Some were painting, others were dancing, and a few were making giant puppets bigger than cars. Facing the water were several quaint cottages, each one framed with different-colored rosebushes.

"Faculty and staff housing," Sunny answered before Olive could ask. "Not everyone lives in the mansion, although it is bigger than a mini-mall." They continued up the path that curved around the island, and Olive admired what appeared to be tiny houses on stilts near the shore. "Guard towers," Sunny explained, "to stop prisoners from escaping. Legend has it that only five managed to make it across the San Francisco Bay, though dozens more tried."

And failed, she didn't have to say. Olive gulped. Well, she wouldn't be escaping across the bay anytime soon. She was still making up her mind about RASCH, but more than that: Olive couldn't swim. Every time her parents or Mimi tried to teach her, it always ended in tears, with Olive having to console them.

She squinted at Yash. If she was to break free from RASCH, it would have to be on BoBu or another boat, she mused. Olive was always thinking of how-tos and what-ifs. She had loved curling up on the couch with Mimi to watch TV and try to solve the mystery on the *Who Done It?* television show before its dramatic conclusion.

Sunny stopped abruptly, her smile turning upside down. They stood before a high chain-link fence topped with rusted barbed wire. The faded DO NOT TRESPASS! sign might have looked imposing at one time, but someone had rewritten it to read: DONUT TRESPASS! and drawn a pair of cheery dancing donuts on it. Now it just looked silly.

The dean's voice softened to a whisper. "After Remy Triste's tragic death, it was discovered that he was deeply in debt. The government seized the property and turned Foggy Island into a prison. To save money, they had prisoners build the cells on the back end of the mansion. But the project was halted before they had a chance to finish." She motioned beyond the DONUT TRESPASS! sign.

"That side of the island is in disarray from almost a hundred years of neglect. When RASCH first began as a school for juvenile offenders, the fence went up to separate the past and present."

Olive peered beyond the barbed wire, eager to check out the disarray, but Sunny was already walking away. Her voice had returned to its chipper tone. "Today, our students are a lively group from all over the world. Each is placed with like-minded others in a pod based on their special skills, like visual arts, theater, music, writing, and other."

Olive was unsure of what her own special skill was, and if she even had one. She would probably be an "other." But first . . .

"Ahem." Olive attempted to sound nonchalant. "Ah— what exactly classifies one as a juvenile offender?"

"Yash!" Sunny boomed, causing her to wince. "Why don't you have a go at the definition?"

Olive had almost forgotten Yash was there. Casting a sullen glance their way, the dean's assistant recited, "A juvenile offender is one who is often unruly, commits status offenses, or is charged with engaging in infractions of the law, such as larceny, vandalism, assault, disorderly conduct, truancy, breaking curfew. . . ."

Olive tried not to cringe. She was guilty of four so far.

Sunny clapped her hands. "Well done, Yash!"

"Humph," Yash replied, slowly edging away from Sunny and Olive as they returned to the mansion. She was about to make a run for it when Sunny stopped her. "Yash, please park Olive's suitcase somewhere while I finish the tour."

After the luggage changed hands, Sunny strode briskly across the yard. Olive had to skip so as not to be left behind.

"Is RASCH still a school for juvenile offenders?" Olive asked. She held her breath.

"Not anymore," Sunny said. Relieved that the academy wasn't some sort of youth detention center, Olive exhaled. "Yet who among us hasn't offended someone else in one way or another? Today's RASCH students have special skills and abilities," the dean continued. "We focus on the present, thus informing the future. Oof!"

Olive nodded, trying to look wise, though she wasn't sure what this statement meant. Mimi used to speak like that, too.

Now Sunny was pointing to the humongous castle that anchored the island. "The deed to Foggy Manor was given to RASCH decades ago by an anonymous benefactor. The upkeep needed for this place is as much as a small kingdom." She gave a sad laugh before perking back up. "In addition to tours, we also host weddings, retreats, parties, and conferences, and just last year, we leased one of the buildings to Butter Bakery!" On cue, a warm breeze delivered the aroma of cinnamon bread, and Olive's mouth watered. "The building was originally the prison bakery, which supplied 'Con Cakes' to stores in San Francisco."

Olive couldn't help but smile. Con Cakes. Mimi, who considered herself a cake connoisseur, would have loved that. Whenever she ordered a cake, which was often, she'd have the bakery write *Congratulations, Olive!* even if they weren't celebrating anything.

Sunny was waving enthusiastically to a group of students who were doing some sort of complicated dance in the gardens. "These days," she informed Olive, "Foggy Manor is most famous for our annual performance fundraiser. Last year, RASCH put on a musical production of *Cats,* and it's still talked about today. I can't tell you what this year's theme is, but I *can* say"—she winked—"ahoy, mate! And here's another hint of what's to come!"

Sunny flung both arms toward a life-sized marble statue of a beautiful woman in a flowing gown, standing proudly in front of the manor. The statue looked oddly familiar to Olive.

"Dame Gloria Vanderwisp," Sunny whispered reverently. "Such a force of nature. Very pertinacious."

"Pertinacious?" Olive asked.

"Yes, strong-willed, tough, resolute. Dame Gloria is a very generous RASCH patron—wealthy up the wazoo! Her family has owned the famed Royal Rumpus necklace for generations. Without her donations, the school would cease to exist! And this year she's personally involved with our fundraiser."

Olive thought about the magazine in Principal Gates's office. No wonder the statue looked familiar—she was the lady with all the jewelry! But what exactly was a Royal Rumpus?

Sunny was now motioning toward a grizzled older man in overalls. His gray hair was thinning, and his face was covered in stubble. "Brood! Yoo-hoo, Brood!" She lowered her head and whispered, "He's our maintenance man," as if letting Olive in on a secret.

Brood walked with a pronounced limp, and his

hands trembled as he leaned a tall ladder against the mansion. He was around Mimi's age when Olive last saw her, but he wasn't nearly as spry as she had been—but then who was? Olive flashed back to her grandmother teaching her how to do handstands and cartwheels. She would give anything for a hug from Mimi right now.

"Currently, Brood is repairing the gargoyles." Sunny motioned up to the handyman. "Several are missing wings and fangs, poor dears. If you need anything fixed, Brood's the one to call!"

Olive wondered if he could fix broken hearts.

5.
LOSER

After they got lost in the meditation gardens and tangled in the flower maze, the dean ended the Foggy Island tour with a rousing "Oof! Oof! Oof!" before dropping Olive off in the cavernous dining hall. "Be sure to try the Butter Bakery cake with your dinner," Sunny said gaily. "It's divine!"

Olive paused at the door, unsure of what would be waiting for her on the other side. So much had happened since breakfast. Too much.

Now that she had stopped walking and talking, Olive was starting to feel exhaustion creep up on her. Emotions swirled like a smoothie in a blender—only instead of strawberries, kiwis, and bananas, hers was made of delight, depression, and confusion. She took a deep breath, then pushed the door open.

Olive's eyes widened. Instead of the green plastic chairs

and wobbly folding tables of her old school, RASCH's dining hall was furnished with fancy long wooden tables and antique chairs with comfy red cushions. Wrought iron chandeliers hung from the high ceilings, and the walls were lined with portraits of snooty-looking RASCH patrons. Each benefactor was painted holding a plate of what Olive imagined to be their favorite food, including oysters, caviar, and toast.

Lively chatter drew Olive deeper into the dining hall, where several students smiled at her for no apparent reason. Gripping her dinner tray of spaghetti, wilted salad, and a thick slice of chocolate cake with orange buttercream frosting, Olive allowed herself to feel a small flicker of hope. Maybe she could actually fit in here. . . .

Then a girl with pastel-pink hair motioned to the back of the room. "Hey, new girl, the loser zone is that way," she said, managing to sound bored and pleased with herself at the same time.

Olive laughed nervously, feeling her insides withering like her salad. Why did she even think this school would be different? But before Olive could say anything, a girl with a killer glare got between them and crossed her arms. "Primrose, who are you calling a loser?"

The pink-haired girl choked on her words. "Not you, Iggy. Her." She pointed to Olive like one points to a hairy spider on the bathroom wall.

"She looks harmless," Iggy said dismissively. She took a step toward Primrose. "Leave her alone, or you'll have to deal with me."

"Thank you," Olive sputtered as Primrose backed away. She was shocked. No one had ever stood up for her before. "Your name is Iggy?"

"Yeah, so what?" Iggy's eyes narrowed. "My full name is Ignatia Amara Inzaghi. You got a problem with that?"

Olive shook her head. She liked the name. "I'm Olive Cobin Zang. Would you like to eat with me?"

"Nope." Iggy returned to a stack of biscuits balanced high on her plate. "Just because I helped you out doesn't make us friends."

Olive's mouth shut like a trap. But before she could apologize—

"Darn it, James, you've made a mess!" It was Primrose again. This time she was pointing dramatically at a boy who had spilled milk on the table in front of him. When Primrose got up, leaving her meal behind, two of her friends, who looked identical except that one had blue hair, the other green, dutifully followed.

James was staring intently at his spilled milk. Though the Reforming Arts School accommodated grades seven to twelve, he looked a little younger, more like a fifth grader. His dark brown Afro was curly on top and short on the sides, in a style that Olive could only dream of. Her own plain black hair was best described as shoulder-length and parted down the middle.

Olive felt a pang of sympathy for James. She knew what it was like to be picked on. Then she was sorry for herself. Having to eat lunch in the cafeteria at her old school was bad enough, but here, Olive would be taking breakfast, lunch, *and* dinner alone in the dining hall.

"It resembles a yeti, or an *Equus asinus asinus.*" James's green-rimmed glasses were either geeky or cool, but Olive wasn't sure which. "*Equus asinus asinus* means 'donkey,'" he explained to anyone who was listening, which was only Olive.

"I didn't know that," she said earnestly. James sized her up as if assessing someone on the witness stand, then launched into a one-way discussion about a ten-thousand-year-old Pesse canoe. Barely listening to him, Olive sat down. Oh, how she wished she could be home with Mimi and a mushroom-and-anchovy pizza.

Exhausted and confused from her peculiar day, Olive pushed the salad aside, skipped the spaghetti, and dove straight into the dessert. It tasted like heaven. With each bite, she could feel her tension melting away. At least there was one thing Olive knew for sure regarding RASCH: it had the best chocolate cake she had ever eaten.

Informed that her dorm assignment would come later, that night Olive found herself alone and lonely in the visitor's quarters. It was an elegant room with a supersoft bed. Olive reminded herself not to get too used to it.

She wondered what her parents were doing now. Did they miss her?

Grudgingly, Olive opened her suitcase to retrieve her pajamas, only to gape in horror.

All her clothes were missing. Her Meggie comics weren't there, either. And worst of all: Olive's diary was nowhere in sight. Instead, she found herself staring at two pairs of sensible black high-heel shoes, bunion splints, a couple of gray suits, white shirts, a fluffy pink bathrobe, and a familiar flannel nightgown—all belonging to her mother.

Olive could not tamp down the queasy feeling that bubbled up. If she had her mother's suitcase, then that meant that Dr. Cobin Zang had hers. Which meant that her mother also had Olive's diary.

She choked back a sob and flung herself onto the bed. Olive had written some horrible things:

Dad is so boring when he's at home.
Mom loves work more than me.
They've abandoned me again.
Sometimes I wish I had different parents!

"I've done it this time," Olive cried into her pillow. By now her parents had probably read her diary. Would they even want to return for her? Who would want such an ungrateful daughter?

Depressed and distressed, Olive had never felt so alone in her life.

The next morning, Olive awoke agitated and with an angry zit on her nose. She had dreamed that her parents had shown up at RASCH, pointed to Primrose, and said cheerfully, "We'll take that one instead."

Olive still had the covers over her head when she heard a slight rustling sound. She sat up to see a slip of paper being pushed under her door.

OLIVE COBIN ZANG, REPORT TO YOUR CONUNDRUM IN THE DEAN'S OFFICE AT 10 A.M. DON'T BE LATE!

She stared at the bold block printing. Conundrum? Was she expected to know what that meant? But her growling stomach made her priorities clear: breakfast first, Conundrum later.

After pulling on yesterday's outfit, Olive tucked the note in her pocket and headed out, backtracking to the dining hall and counting six, seven . . . eight looming portraits of Dame Gloria. Each was painted for a decade of her life, and though she was gorgeous in all of them, each successive image captured her looking slightly more aloof.

Olive rounded the corner and came across several rooms along the next hall, which was lavishly decorated with wild-life paintings encased in gold frames that stretched from floor to ceiling. The Scrivener Writing Room was crowded with cushy couches and squishy beanbag chairs. And the Artsy Gaggle Studio was lined with blank canvases resting on easels.

The scent of fresh-baked bread pulled Olive into the dining hall, and the sight of assorted breakfast pastries on buffet tables instantly lifted her spirits. She put three on her plate.

The scary girl, Iggy, was sitting in the same place as the night before. She caught Olive's eye and nodded, just barely. "You got your Conundrum today?" Iggy asked, though she said it more like an statement.

James sat nearby, a book in one hand and a muffin in the other. He looked up at Olive with interest.

Even though she was not a morning person, Olive pretended to be one. "As a matter of fact, I am scheduled for a Conundrum," she said in what she hoped was a lighthearted and conversational tone. She sat down across from James and picked up her blueberry muffin. "Oh my gosh, *thisissogood!*" Olive blurted out through a mouthful. She took a couple more bites of her pastry before asking, "What is a Conundrum?"

Iggy pushed her jagged dark bangs aside to reveal ice-blue eyes. She explained gruffly, "It's everything, and different for everyone. Your results determine your placement at RASCH, or if you're even RASCH material. I've heard that several students had to leave before they even started going to class here."

Olive set her muffin down. She wasn't hungry anymore. Where would she even go if she failed her Conundrum?! When her parents were on their business trips, it was impossible to get ahold of them. Would Sunny let her stay until they got back?

"You going to eat that?" James was eyeing Olive's muffin. She handed it over. "You'll be told that there are no wrong answers for the Conundrum," he said helpfully. "However, I can tell you that they're on the lookout for irreconcilable differences between you and RASCH."

"What does that even mean?" Olive was so confused.

"It means you'd better not mess up," Iggy said, slipping a butter knife into her pocket. "Good luck. You're going to need it."

6.
DONUT TRESPASS!

A Conundrum was a test—Olive figured as much. Tragically, she had never done well on tests, especially those where you had to fill in the bubbles. Questions like: "If Beatrice has five donuts and offers two to Timmy, how many does she have left?" What if Timmy didn't like donuts but was more of a Pop-Tart person? Where was the bubble for that?

There was still over an hour before the mysterious Conundrum, so Olive set out for a walk around the island. Mimi swore that walks were a great way to calm down and find yourself, which Olive never quite understood. Why would you want to find yourself if you aren't missing? The thought of her grandmother brought a faint smile to Olive's face, even as it made her chest ache.

It was a sunny day, and the wind made ripples over the ocean that reminded Olive of her favorite wavy potato chips. Not far from the dock was a boathouse painted in weathered hues of blue and green, and it was home to several boats, including BoBu, the boat bus that brought her here.

Nearby, the Foggy Island General Store was housed in what looked like an enchanted cottage from the fairy-tale books Mimi used to read to Olive. Though it appeared small on the outside, Olive was delighted by the inside. The shop seemed to go on forever, packed with school supplies, books, snacks, and Foggy Island souvenirs.

The display near the cash register held an array of snow globes. Olive reached for a Foggy Manor one. She shook it, watching the fake snowflakes whirl around the mansion before settling at the base. The last thing Olive needed was another snow globe. She gently returned it to the shelf.

Next door the aroma of warm bread, cakes, and cookies spilled out of the tidy brick Butter Bakery building, beckoning Olive through its red door. Behind the counter, a woman with a mess of black hair tucked under her tall chef's hat looked up at Olive. Nearby an older lady dumped a bag of flour into a huge mixing bowl, causing it to poof and create a cloud around her.

"Shouldn't you be in school?" the younger woman asked in a British accent.

"I'm new to RASCH and have my Conundrum soon," Olive told her, taking in the cookies spread across a large marble table.

The baker nodded knowingly and picked up one decorated like a monarch butterfly. "Then you shall need this to fortify yourself."

"Thank you," Olive said politely. The cookie almost looked too pretty to eat. "Did you make last night's chocolate cake and this morning's muffins?"

"Indeed!" The baker blushed. "I'm Poppy, owner of Butter Bakery, and that's Auntie Winnie."

Her assistant, who was now covered with a light dusting of flour, waved shyly. Auntie Winnie reminded Olive of a sweet, quiet grandma who knitted, rather than her own Mimi, who said things like, "If you get tired from hanging by your arms and think you're going to fall, hang by your legs."

Auntie Winnie motioned to Poppy. "She was a finalist on *The Big British Baking Battle*," she said proudly.

Poppy shrugged like it was no big deal. "I was gobsmacked when it happened! Simply gobsmacked!"

Gobsmacked. Olive liked that word. A baking superstar right here on Foggy Island? At least if Olive was forced to attend RASCH, there would be pastries. However, she needed more than a cookie, no matter how lovely it was, to take her mind off her abandonment and the impending Conundrum.

As Olive left Butter Bakery and continued to explore, an unexpected gust of wind swept away her sense of foreboding. Outside, RASCHers and their instructors were giving off electric sparks of energy and creativity, and it was contagious. On a great expanse of lawn, circles of students scribbled furiously in notebooks. Some wrote with feather quill pens. When their teacher slapped his chest and roared,

"Write what's in your heart!" several students responded with an enthusiastic *"Oof!"*

Olive found herself laughing. She had never known a school like this. It seemed more like her summers at Mimi's acrobatics camps, where "controlled chaos" was the order of the day. There, she and her grandmother had trained in the tricks of the trapeze, tightrope, and other acrobatics. Mimi would pass on her wise words, including "Balance is important," "Go with the flow," and "It's essential to develop trust."

"I trust you," Olive would shout as she swung back and forth on the trapeze. Even when they were high in the air and the safety net seemed miles away, Olive had never felt so free.

"Yes, but"—Mimi was upside down, too, with her legs hooked onto another trapeze bar—"you also need to trust yourself." She swung in Olive's direction. "Listen to your instincts. When you're ready, let go. I'll catch you!"

Never once did Mimi let Olive fall.

On another part of Foggy Island, a group was taking turns tucking themselves inside giant inflatable tires and rolling each other around a statue of Dame Gloria cradling a cat. The RASCH version of PE?

At her old school, PE meant wearing unattractive blue shorts and getting yelled at by teammates who only cared about winning at softball or soccer. No one appreciated that Olive could walk a tightrope or do double aerial cartwheels.

The more Olive observed, the more she noticed how happy everyone seemed at RASCH. Not even the teachers looked bored. Oh, sure, there were a couple of scowlers—but weren't there always?

If school was a must, Olive admitted that this was the sort of place she might like. As she considered it, getting through the Conundrum started to feel less and less like a chore and more and more like a challenge. Anticipation, eagerness, and anxiety collided in Olive's stomach, leaving her iffy and uncertain.

By the time she made it to the DONUT TRESPASS! sign, her scrumptious Butter Bakery cookie was practically gone. Wind whistled in her ears, and she squinted through the holes of the chain-link fence. Why was the area closed off? What didn't they want people to see?

Olive glanced furtively toward the mansion, where most of the teachers and students were. Maybe she'd just take a quick peek. Making sure no one was watching, Olive quickly crawled through a break near the bottom of the fence. She was sure her parents wouldn't approve, but they weren't here, were they? Mimi, though, would have encouraged Olive. She would've said, "It's better to apologize after than to ask permission before."

Once past the fence, Olive brushed herself off. She immediately felt a strange calm and quiet. Already, she could see that the back of Foggy Manor was in ruins. Rusted machinery had sunk into the ground, and there were mountains of bricks that looked ready to topple. The shell of an airplane was surrounded by stacks of old, worn-down prison gates.

This didn't resemble anything like the front of the opulent mansion, with its manicured lawns and topiary gardens. Here, gangly trees, bramblebushes, and gnarly weeds reminded her of the forest of thorns that surrounded Sleeping Beauty's castle. Above it all, at the top of a hill, was a shuttered red lighthouse that must have been majestic in its glory days. Olive itched to explore it, but she pushed away the urge. First she had a Conundrum to conquer.

As she went back toward the hole in the fence, some movement caught her eye. She turned to find a regal white swan sailing along the narrow moat around Foggy Manor. It was followed by a black swan and a swarm of light gray babies.

Olive was delighted. *Baby swans!* She'd adored swans ever since Mimi had read her *The Ugly Duckling* when she was younger. Olive always identified with the Ugly Duckling. As the swans swam to greet her, she bent over to toss some cookie crumbs their way.

"Enjoy!" was the last word Olive uttered before tumbling headfirst into the murky moat.

Panic set in as she plunged into the dark, cold, unforgiving water. Olive flailed, gasping. "I can't swim!" she wanted to cry. The scream lodged in her throat. She plunged below the surface twice more before her feet found solid ground, and she rapidly stood up. It didn't matter that the water only reached the middle of her chest. When you were thrashing

around, it felt the same whether it was three feet deep or three hundred feet.

Alarmed, the swans had scattered, leaving Olive all alone, trying to catch her breath and feeling relieved that no one saw her panic. Drenched, she dragged herself out of the moat and hurriedly slogged toward Foggy Manor, leaving a trail of puddles and shame behind her.

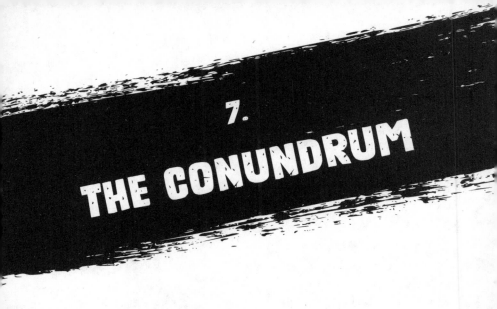

7.
THE CONUNDRUM

Before arriving at her Conundrum, Olive was forced to choose between wearing her sopping-wet clothes or something of her mother's. As she rushed from her room, she caught a glimpse of her reflection in the mirror. The oversized gray wool suit gave Olive the distinct impression that she was shrinking. Maybe she was. But what choice did she have? It was either the suit or her mother's red flannel nightgown.

Having hurried to the dean's office, Olive was out of time and out of breath. Any dreams she'd had about sitting on the lawn and laughing with her RASCH teachers had drowned when she fell into the moat. She could only hope they wouldn't kick her out before she had even started.

"Three minutes late!" a voice bellowed from behind the massive mahogany desk that guarded Sunny's office door.

Piles of papers were stacked so high that Olive couldn't see Yash until she came around to the front. The woman lowered her goggles and gave Olive's clothes the once-over. "Fascinating look," Yash noted wryly.

Olive grimaced and attempted to smooth down her sticky, wet hair. She was about to apologize when Sunny flung open her door. "Olive, come in, come in! Are you ready?"

"Not at all," Olive answered honestly, tottering toward her. How did anyone walk in high heels?

"Not to worry." Sunny fluttered her fingers, shutting her office door behind Olive and Yash. "No one ever is."

Sunny's office looked like a smaller, brighter version of the manor's halls. One wall was crammed with abstract paintings of Sunny—by RASCH students, perhaps? The opposite wall held a single oversized oil portrait of Dame Gloria posed like the *Mona Lisa* but draped in jewels like a queen on coronation day, and with a cat brooch on her sash. A huge hourglass rested on the window ledge and—

Boom! Without warning, Yash flipped the hourglass and slammed it on the table, causing Olive to jump. The Conundrum had commenced.

"Olive," Sunny began seriously, "what's your favorite animal?"

Is there a right answer to this? Olive wondered wildly. ". . . Baby swans?"

"Where would you like to go on Tuesday?" Sunny continued, not missing a beat.

Olive's heart lurched. "Home."

As Sunny lobbed questions, Yash recorded Olive's answers in a large leather-bound book.

"Answer faster," Sunny sang. "Don't think."

Olive thought about this. *That* was odd, wasn't it? "Don't think" was the opposite of what teachers told her to do at her old school.

"Whom do you admire?"

"Mimi."

"If your name wasn't Olive, what would it be?"

"Olive."

"What word describes you?"

"Misfit."

"Would you rather save a rain forest or go on a luxury vacation?"

"Save a rain forest."

"Do you get scared?"

"Yes."

"Are you still nervous?"

"Not so much."

The faster the questions came, the calmer Olive grew. She hardly had time to take a breath when Yash handed her a green notebook and a pencil that was so sharp it could have been classified as a weapon.

"Now then . . ." Sunny popped a lemon drop into her mouth. She offered one to Olive. It was more sour than expected, but Olive appreciated the jolt of tartness. "Please draw all you can remember about Foggy Manor, Foggy Island, and the people you met. You have twenty minutes. *Go!*"

With considerable effort, Yash turned the heavy bronze hourglass upside down yet again. As the sand began to sift, Olive swiftly opened the notebook to a blank page. Without hesitation, she got to work, quickly drawing Yash's rain slicker, boots, and goggles, and BoBu, the amphibious vehicle. She included details like the stubble on Brood's solemn face and the flowers in Sunny's hair. From there, wide, sweeping sketches of the manor's exterior and the prison guard towers made it onto the pages. James, Iggy, and Primrose and her friends, too. She skipped the desolate side of the island, the moat, and the swans.

"Time!" Yash shouted.

Startled, Olive dropped her pencil.

Sunny took the notebook and turned the pages in silence, her face blank. It was impossible to tell what she was thinking. Olive squelched the urge to fidget, instead massaging her hand, which was sore from gripping her pencil too tight. At last, the dean looked up and beamed. "You even got the gargoyles. No one ever remembers them, poor dears. Great job!"

Relieved, Olive allowed herself to relax . . . until Yash approached her with a blindfold. There was more?

"Put this on," Olive was instructed, "and then reach into the bag and identify what's in it." Yash held up a burlap sack that had something moving around inside.

As the Conundrum stretched into the afternoon, it got increasingly more challenging and creative. Olive had been expecting grammar and math questions, but other than Sunny asking, "How many feet are between that wall and this desk?" there were none.

Regardless, Olive was exhausted when she reached the end of her Conundrum. She had no clue how she'd done, but she knew she had tried her very best, as Mimi had always encouraged her to do.

As Sunny pored over Olive's Conundrum, Yash kicked back in an armchair, swinging her feet while enjoying the sports section of a newspaper. She handed Olive the front page to keep herself busy while she waited, but Olive was too nervous to read. She put the front page down, catching a glimpse of the headline "JEWELRY CRIME SPREE RAMPS UP" and a small "KITTYKON IS COMING YOUR WAY!" ad.

As drained as she was after the mystifying Conundrum, Olive also felt more alive than she had in a long time. By now, she wanted to pass the test more than anything. Maybe even more than going home.

Finally, the dean put her pen down. "Yash, will you please escort our candidate out?"

Panic stabbed at Olive from all angles before Sunny broke into a smile. "Olive Cobin Zang, congratulations on your most excellent Conundrum! Your quick wit, honesty, and powers of deductive, inductive, and reductive reasoning were stellar. *Oof!*"

Olive gasped. "I can stay?!"

"We would be honored if you did!" Sunny's voice was melodic. She shook Olive's hand vigorously. "For now, you will take lessons and reside with the other RASCHers of pod 101. It's . . . an interesting group, what's left of them." Olive detected a mischievous twinkle in her eyes. "Your teachers are looking for a very specific kind of student, and I think we found her."

Olive let go of an "oof." She had been accepted into RASCH!

8.
MODEST & MONICA

Olive had never looked forward to school before. She found that she quite liked the feeling. Yash was winding through corridors, and Olive could have sworn they went through the same ones more than once. "Where are we going?" She was eager to find out.

"You'll know when you get there," Yash finally replied as she skidded to a stop in front of a huge door that was fortified with wrought iron. She pounded both fists against the solid wood. "New one coming in!" Yash shouted, then took off, leaving Olive to begin her first day of class on her own.

Pod 101 had a wing of rooms all to themselves in an isolated part of Foggy Manor. The door creaked as it slowly swung open on its own. Tentatively, Olive stepped inside. Instantly, she felt at ease, even though it was unlike any classroom she'd ever been in.

Marble pillars held up the towering ceiling. Elaborately carved tables with throne-like chairs faced a whiteboard in the front. When everyone turned her way, Olive waved shyly at Iggy and James . . . and was bummed to see Primrose and her two friends, who were wearing identical sweaters, only one twin's had "Enid" embroidered on it and the other's said "Ethel."

There was an imposing couple near the whiteboard. The man looked delighted to see her standing in the doorway.

"Olive!" His voice was warm and kind, and he spoke with a lyrical Russian accent. "Welcome! I'm Modest Cusak, one half of your pod 101 leader team." He gestured to the woman standing next to him. "The other half is my partner and wife, the famous Monica LaMonica."

Modest's towering stature and bulging muscles reminded Olive of an action figure. Monica, on the other hand, had tortured her jet-black hair into a tight bun. She wore a tank top that showed off athletic arms, and her complicated camouflage pants were tucked into heavy black boots.

Olive's eyes lit up. She had never seen a teacher dressed like this. The only bright color Monica wore was a slash of cherry-red lipstick, dramatic against her white skin. When she spoke, it was with an accent Olive couldn't identify.

"Modest and I will be your teachers and trainers." Her voice was clipped. "You will do what we say and not ask questions."

Modest clasped his huge hands together and brought them to his heart. "What Monica means is that we would like you to follow our instructions. If they are unclear, then we encourage you to ask questions, interact, be involved! After all, here at the Reforming Arts School, we are all about finding our true selves."

In a fluid motion, Monica retrieved a knife from her boot. Olive tensed. She imagined the knife being thrown at her before she even had a chance to sit down. But then Monica pulled an apple out of another pocket and began to peel it. Relieved, Olive found the courage to ask, "Excuse me, but what happens in pod 101?"

Monica laughed, not unkindly. "Modest, tell the girl."

Modest knelt in front of Olive, who was still standing, and looked at her solemnly. "You will have general studies, like math, and science, and English, but they will be targeted at you reaching your full potential. And, of course, there will be boxing and ballet." He pointed proudly to Monica

LaMonica. "Meet the two-time lightweight boxing champion of the world!"

"Oh, Modest, please stop!" Monica shook her head but looked delighted as she tossed the unbroken apple peel over her shoulder. It landed neatly in the trash bin. "Modest Cusak," Monica said, pointing her knife at him, "is a world-class Russian ballet dancer, known for his signature move—lifting TWO ballerinas aloft while dancing!"

Modest produced a worn photo from his jumpsuit pocket. "All of you will be immersed in performing and reforming arts," he explained, holding the image high so everyone could see. "We aim to tap into your inner soul to make you well rounded, independent, and courageous!"

This reminded Olive of her parents when they tried to explain what they did for a living. She was never quite sure what they were talking about. Olive was directed to sit at a table next to Zeke, a boy with windswept caramel-colored hair who looked like he could be a TV star. When he nodded at her, Olive coughed nervously. She wondered if he was staring at her zit.

James scooted his chair over to Olive and whispered, "Nice suit, but too big." He was wearing pressed slacks, a collared shirt under a vest, and a blue bow tie with red umbrellas.

Nearby, a girl Olive didn't recognize kept tapping her fingers on an invisible keyboard, causing the large rings on her fingers to glow orange like her headscarf. Olive wondered if she wore the rings to match her headscarf, or if she wore the headscarf to match the rings.

"Philomena," Modest gently reminded the girl, "no computers unless it's tech time."

Philomena obliged, clenching her fingers into a fist so that her rings stopped glowing. Olive's jaw nearly dropped. Were her rings really *computers*? She'd never seen computers so small!

Across the room, a friendly boy with a mass of curly brown hair gave Olive a cheerful nod, as if they were already friends. In return, she offered an awkward smile, then tugged self-consciously at her mother's wool skirt. Her hair was nearly dry now, but when Olive tried to smooth it, her hand came away with moss, leaves, and a swan feather.

To Olive's right, Iggy was making a big show of wrinkling her nose. "You smell bad," she said, getting up and moving to another table.

That familiar feeling of humiliation greeted Olive. Trying not to bring attention to herself, she sniffed her armpit and was horrified to find that she smelled like murky moat water and moss. Olive's eyes scanned the room to see if anyone else had noticed, but everyone was busy talking.

Monica LaMonica raised an eyebrow, and instantly the class went silent. "Tomorrow is the big day," she said, walking to the rear of the classroom. "I hope you're ready for the Gymkhana Splore!"

"Gymkhana Splore?" Olive repeated aloud.

From the far side of the room, Monica LaMonica answered, "Splore is what sets you apart and binds you together. Gymkhana is where it takes place."

Olive's mouth snapped shut. *How did she hear me from all the way back there?*

"Not to worry," Modest assured everyone. "No one has ever died during the Gymkhana Splore!"

"There's always a first time," Monica pointed out.

Olive hoped that Monica was joking, and joined in laughing with the other students. Philomena turned to her and gave her a kind smile.

Olive returned the smile. Maybe, finally, this was a place where she could fit in.

9.

BALLYHOO

After school, everyone scattered. Having gotten past the Conundrum and been placed in a pod, Olive felt a lightness in her step that had been absent since the news of Mimi. She was eager to see the dormitory—and to take a bath. The wool suit was making her itchy.

Upon entering her room, she stood stunned. Olive double-checked her paperwork to make sure she was in the right place. There was a canopy bed fit for a princess—it had more puffy pillows than she knew what to do with—and a stately purple armchair with gold tassels awaited her in the corner. Forest-green wallpaper awash with pink roses covered the walls. And thick red velvet curtains parted to reveal a stunning view of the bay and the San Francisco skyline, and . . . Were those whales swimming in the water?

Dr. Cobin Zang's orange suitcase was already waiting in

her new room, next to an oversized antique wardrobe. Olive started to climb into it—like she had read about in a book—when she heard "Hello?"

The cautious voice came from the doorway. Olive spun around to find Philomena holding a gift basket. "This is from Sunny."

Olive hesitated, unsure. At her last school, the PE teacher had once said, "I have a present for you," and then made Olive run an extra lap because she couldn't catch a fly ball.

Philomena nudged the basket toward Olive. "We all got one on our first day. Oh, and you can call me Phil. That's what all my friends call me. Well, if I had friends, that's what I'd want them to call me."

"Thank you, Phil." Olive peered inside the basket and admired the generous assortment of Foggy Island pens and pencils, notebooks, a RASCH brochure that included a glossy photo of Dame Gloria Vanderwisp captioned *Our Esteemed Premier Patron,* and a pink box of Butter Bakery cookies.

But the best part wasn't in the basket. It was when Phil asked, rather bashfully, "Want to join me for dinner?"

"I would love that!" Olive answered so loudly that it startled both of them.

As they headed to the dining hall, Olive silently scolded herself for being a dork. At least Phil didn't seem to mind and instead was talking about pens. "Did you know that the average one can write forty-five thousand words without running out of ink?"

"I wonder what the average word length is,"

Olive said. Words like "conundrum" would throw off the average.

"James would know," Phil told her. The sounds of students talking and silverware clinking got louder as they neared the dining hall. She waved her hand, giving Olive another flash of her rings. "He knows everything. Let's ask him."

"Will you, um, also show me how your rings work?" Olive asked cautiously. She didn't want to sound too nosy.

"Oh, Olive, I would love to!" Phil practically screamed. But just as Olive gave her a grin, Phil's bright smile fell. "You must think I'm a dork."

Olive laughed. "I was thinking you thought the same thing about me!"

"Maybe we can be dorks together," Phil suggested.

"Like Meggie and Elise," Olive proclaimed. "They're total dorks and don't care who knows!"

Phil stopped walking and shook her head.

"It's a comic book," Olive quickly explained. *"Meggie & Her Fun Family . . ."*

"Meggie?"

Olive thought she had blown it, until Phil grabbed her arm. "Meggie's my favorite! I have most of the comics and even brought them with me to RASCH!"

Olive let out a squeal, and then the two went in search of James.

The Gymkhana Splore was just as much of a conundrum as, well, the Conundrum. In class the next morning, James raised both hands high like he was surrendering. "How were we supposed to study for this?" he asked, a frantic edge in his voice.

"You can't study for the Gymkhana Splore," Monica said bluntly. She was roaming the room like a lion on the prowl. Olive expected her to pounce at any moment. "Either you're good at it or you aren't."

"But what exactly *is* Gymkhana Splat?" Primrose demanded. Ethel and Enid looked at her admiringly.

"Splore," Iggy muttered. "Get it right."

James pushed up his glasses. "Everyone knows that 'gymkhana' is a British Raj term for a place where skill-based contests are held. 'Splore' is Scottish for 'frolic.' Therefore, I'm assuming we're going somewhere for a field day?"

Modest applauded. Olive nodded as she wrote down what James had just said. Iggy muttered sarcastically, "Is there anything you don't know?"

"I don't even know why *you're* here," James muttered back.

"How is this different from the Conundrum?" Primrose pressed.

Modest scrunched up his nose. "I can see how it would be confusing. The Conundrum helped find your proper pod placement. Now that you're here, you will have a splore, which is a dexterity challenge that takes place in the gymkhana."

Monica added, "The Gymkhana Splore will test your physical and mental abilities—"

"So expect *lots* of ballyhoo!" Modest enthused as he leaped around the room. For someone so big, he was surprisingly light on his feet.

James raised his hand again. "How will we be graded? Is there extra credit?"

"There's much more at stake than just grades," Monica said mysteriously. "Much, much more."

Olive's heart sank. She'd hoped that grades wouldn't be a big deal at RASCH. In the past, she'd gotten low marks on tests for not showing her work—even if her answers were correct.

Monica stopped by her desk and seemed startled by Olive's messy notes. Olive cringed—handwriting had never been her strong suit. When Monica held up her notebook for all to see, she braced herself for criticism.

"This!" Monica announced. "I like that Olive is doing this. Class, from now on, I want each of you to develop a secret code that only you can read."

Olive sat up taller. All right, maybe if there *were* grades, they wouldn't be too bad.

The class left the room, with Modest Cusak leading the way to the gymkhana, sometimes leaping, often pirouetting, but mostly strutting. Monica brought up the rear to make sure no one got lost or tried to escape. On several occasions, she had to stop Olive from exploring random stairwells and sternly remind her to "stay with the group!"

Pod 101 wound through corridors, up and down stairs, and around and around the building, inside and out. The pastel-haired girls began to complain, and they refused to stop until Iggy accidentally-on-purpose bumped into Primrose, making her stumble into Enid and Ethel, who apologized for being in her way.

At last, Modest halted in front of a solid metal door that loomed at least twelve feet high. Rusted suits of armor guarded either side.

"When Remy Triste created Foggy Manor, he had several oversized ballrooms built." Monica held up a heavy black key. "This is one of ours."

10.
GYMKHANA SPLORE

The students entered chattering but one by one fell silent in awe upon seeing the gymkhana for the first time. It resembled a cross between an arena, a dance hall, and an athletic club. Richly colored walls encircled the stadium-sized venue. There was an aboveground pool spilling over with colorful balls, and in one corner a machine that looked more steampunk than cutting-edge was churning out bubbling green ooze.

Overhead, long swatches of sturdy, brightly hued fabric cascaded from high chandeliers, reminding Olive of the aerial silks at her grandmother's. At the sight of them, a familiar fluttery feeling embraced her. It was the combination of excitement and anxiety that she got when Mimi taught her new acrobatics. In that moment, Olive missed her grandmother more than ever.

Tracksuits with their names on them spun around on a motorized clothing rack near the door, and boxes of brand-new sneakers were stacked high. As the students changed in the nearby locker rooms, Olive was relieved to shed her mother's clothes.

After they were suitably attired, the students were instructed to begin stretching. Olive took deep, soothing breaths like Mimi had taught her. She wanted to impress Monica and Modest, and to show Phil and the others that she was worthy of their friendship. But more than anything, Olive wanted to prove to herself that she could do this.

She soon discovered that the Gymkhana Splore would be the most strenuous and demanding trial she'd ever faced. They were all put through a battery of challenges across the gymkhana, a few at a time. Since splores took place in rotation, those who were not on deck were told to play board games. Olive liked Clue the best, and after she successfully deduced that the murderer was Colonel Mustard with a wrench in the Billiard Room, Ethel flipped the board over. "Oops," she said, smiling sweetly.

When Olive's splore team was called, she was paired with Enid, Iggy, and Zeke, the boy with the good hair. For their first challenge, Modest asked, "Can you do this?" He leaped effortlessly, spun around, and landed softly ten feet away. "Or how about this?" From a running position, Modest vaulted across the gymkhana and over a chair with his arms spread like an eagle's wings.

Olive watched as Zeke nailed the leap. Iggy got the height but landed hard. Then it was Olive's turn, and for a moment she couldn't move. What if she failed all the splores? Would *that* get her kicked out of RASCH?

She was just starting to think she could be very happy here.

"You all right, Olive?" There was concern in Modest's voice. "You don't have to do anything you don't want to."

Olive shook off her angst as she remembered what Mimi always said: "As long as you try, you're a success."

"I want to," she said, sounding confident, even though that wasn't what she felt inside.

On the first attempt, Olive ran into the chair. On the second, she tripped over herself. On the third, she cleared the chair, then fell. When Enid laughed, Olive got up and laughed, too, despite feeling mortified. "I'll just have to do better," she said, more to herself than the others.

"That's the spirit!" Modest enthused.

When it came time for the fabric dangling from the chandeliers, Olive steeled herself, then soared. She sprang up from atop a table to grab a velvet fabric swatch and shimmied up with the ease of someone who'd practiced this all her life in her grandmother's backyard tent. While fifteen feet off the ground, instead of getting hopelessly tangled like her teammates, she gained enough momentum to swing from one chandelier to another, before executing a graceful swan dive into the ball pit.

When she emerged, Phil was applauding, and Olive thought she even saw a flicker of a smile from Monica.

The final splore was the most complicated; no longer in teams, all the students were to take the challenge at once. It was an obstacle course that consisted of a peril pit, waterworks, a stink room, and buttered monkey bars. Zeke was immediately in front with the long, smooth strides of a track star. Primrose and the twins were behind him, shoving anyone in their path, followed closely by James, Iggy, a lanky boy called Theo, plus three others Olive couldn't name. Bringing up the rear were Phil and Olive, who kept encouraging each other.

Zeke's fearless headfirst dive into the peril pit resulted in an impressive purple bump on his forehead. More important, it revealed that the pit's deep depth was an optical illusion. Then, by listening carefully to Primrose's complaining, Olive knew to avoid the sharp left turns that led out of the waterworks and straight into sticky walls. And in the stink room, as she marveled at Iggy's determination to power through without gagging, James stopped cold.

"The *smell*!" he shrieked, arms straight by his sides, fists clenched.

Even though she was almost out of the dungeon-like chamber, Iggy turned around just as Olive caught up to James. Her eyes started watering. He was right—it *did* stink.

Olive held her breath as she and Iggy dragged James past barrels of sliced durian, the smelliest fruit in the world. By the time they joined Theo and Phil at the monkey bars, everyone else was a mess, having slipped off the greased monkey bars and into the mud below. Primrose, Enid, and Ethel were fighting each other about how to best get across, and one boy had quit.

"We'll never make it across by ourselves," Iggy observed bitterly.

"If only the monkey bars weren't so slippery," Olive thought out loud.

"That's it!" Theo said, still holding his nose. "We should use the waterworks on the monkey bars!"

The three of them rushed back to divert the waterworks and blast the grease off the monkey bars. Then Olive, Theo, and Iggy crossed the monkey bars, avoided the mud, and dove over the finish line as a team.

Olive had never felt so drained—or so happy.

Afterward, the students were allowed a quick lunch break while Modest and Monica huddled. James wandered over to Olive, Iggy, and Theo, who were reliving their triumph.

"You guys were really good," he said, biting into his second slice of pizza. He pushed his glasses up on his nose, and Olive bit back a smile at the praise.

"Nice knowing you losers!" Primrose pointed to Olive's group. "We saw you helping each other. Maybe we ought to let Modest and Monica know that you were *cheating*! You'll probably get expelled for that."

"What's your problem?" Iggy was holding a banana. In her hand, it looked like a dangerous weapon.

Primrose and her groupies quickly scattered, but they left Olive unnerved. She had already been expelled from school once. Olive had started a fight—or at least that's what went on her permanent record. She was trying to protect a younger student who was being picked on by bullies. It took both her parents to convince Principal Gates to let Olive back in school at the time, even though Olive insisted it wasn't necessary.

RASCH, though, was unlike any school Olive

had ever heard of. Foggy Island was way better than the video, and the mansion with its turrets and grand rooms was like a fairy-tale castle. Olive had aced the Conundrum, and the Gymkhana Splore reminded her of the acrobatics she did with Mimi. Monica and Modest were beyond great. And talking Meggie comics with Phil, hanging out with the others—well, that was the very best part. Olive held tightly to her new memories and waited uneasily for Modest and Monica to come to their decision about everyone's fate.

11.
TOP SECRET

Monica LaMonica paced silently. Modest Cusak's normally cheerful demeanor was muted. Sunny had arrived in a bright pink caftan and was trying unsuccessfully to blend in with the dark curtains. Next to her, Yash wielded a clipboard and kept clicking her pen, seemingly unaware of how annoying it was.

"Attention, please!" Modest sounded serious. The class quieted immediately. "Based on the results of the Gymkhana Splore, we have decided to divide this pod."

A wave of discomfort ebbed through the room. Olive's chest tightened. She crossed her fingers, then noticed Phil doing the same. The mean girls looked smug, and when Primrose mouthed "Cheater" to Olive, her stomach pretzeled.

Monica held up a list. "Will the following students please stand."

Olive froze. Primrose and the twins were selected, and

Zeke, of course, plus three others. The only ones still seated were Olive, James, Phil, Theo, and Iggy, all looking like they had just read the scene in *Meggie & Her Fun Family* where Meggie's dog, Rufus, had eaten too many donuts and was gravely ill.

Sunny stepped forward and opened her arms. "Those standing, please come with me. You will be placed in new pods according to your talents. Those seated will remain here in pod 101 with Modest Cusak and Monica LaMonica."

Huh? Olive blinked in confusion and watched the other group exit. Swiftly, Modest locked the door and pushed a heavy table against it while Monica bolted the windows and closed the curtains.

"What I am about to say is top secret," Monica LaMonica began in a low voice. "*Top secret*—do you all understand?"

Eyes wide, the group nodded in unison. Olive felt woozy and was glad they were already sitting down.

However, Monica didn't seem upset. Instead, she looked pleased.

"You five are exceptional. Your unique skills, attitudes, and attributes—off the charts!"

Olive opened her mouth, but no words came out. The others looked just as stunned. It was Iggy who finally found her voice. "So . . . we're not in trouble for helping each other during the Gymkhana Splore?"

Modest pointed to her with both hands. "Extra points for that! No one said it was a competition. Some just assumed it was."

Olive's thoughts were jumbled. Zeke was clearly the best, yet where was he?

"How was this calculated?" James looked suspicious.

"The splores counted for thirty-seven percent of your scores," Monica explained. "Forty-one percent went to camaraderie, fair play, and integrity."

Modest jumped in. "Thirty-nine percent went to your skills at . . . board games!"

Board games?

"That's a hundred and seventeen percent," Iggy quickly added.

While Modest counted on his fingers, Monica cleared her throat. "Yes, well, a hundred and seventeen percent is what we want you to give us. Welcome to our supersecret team! You have been selected to join an elite force of specially trained operatives and will receive the full intel on Monday."

By now, Olive's head was spinning. She didn't even know what to think. She didn't even know where to *begin* thinking.

"Awesome!" Iggy pumped her fist in the air. "So, are we like spies? Or maybe a reconnaissance team?"

"Monday!" Modest leaped and landed next to her. He began to plié. "All your questions will be answered then."

James raised his hand. "Do we get secret names so no one knows who we are?"

"No one knows who we are already," Theo said helpfully.

"The people who matter know who you are," Monica assured them.

"Monday," Modest repeated as he continued his pliés. "In the meantime, play board games. Rest and relax, and then get ready."

Ready for what? Was this even for real? Olive half expected someone to appear from behind the curtain and say it was all a prank. Before she could ask, Modest and Monica dragged the heavy table away from the door and exited the room, leaving the five students to ponder what had just happened.

James was the first to break the silence. "We're supposed to play board games, so I pick Battleship." Each of the remaining pod 101 team members chose one game they wanted to play, and given that there were two hours until dinner, Iggy calculated that they had twenty-four minutes per game. Then James insisted that a bathroom break be worked in, and Theo suggested time to stretch and chat after each round. Now they were at twenty minutes per game, leaving Phil to wonder if that was truly enough time. To hurry things along, Olive offered to forgo Clue, her favorite, so they could have twenty-five minutes each for four games, plus a bathroom break, plus time to chat.

In the final minutes of speed-Monopoly, James yelled at Iggy, who was trying to trick Theo into giving her his Get Out of Jail Free card. Later, during three-board Scrabble, Olive ended up with all consonants. "I think this is maybe a word?" she said, her voice shaky. Her tiles spelled "CRWTHS."

Phil and Iggy were quick to challenge her but were bowled

over to discover they were wrong when they consulted the official Scrabble dictionary. They both lost their turns as punishment.

Theo nudged Olive. "You knew it was a word, didn't you?"

"Maybe, maybe not" was all she'd admit, smiling.

"Well played," Theo said approvingly.

Battleship was traditionally a two-player game, but James created a multiple-player version for all of them. His strategy, Olive noted, was not just firing at the center, but also watching where his opponents were looking to gauge their moves. James won in a quick eight minutes. When he suggested they play again with their remaining time, he was outvoted. Iggy wanted to use the extra time to play Jenga.

"Technically, it's not a board game," James quickly said.

"Technically, you're annoying," she replied.

After a four-to-one vote, Iggy combined several Jenga games to make it more difficult, and the resulting tower of wooden blocks was taller than James.

As the clock ticked toward dinner, Iggy started pushing the others to hurry so a winner could be declared. With a steady hand, Phil expertly removed pieces, making sure the tower still stood. Theo and Olive were swift and methodical with their choices, and James still seemed agitated that no one wanted another game of Battleship.

"Come on, James," Iggy chided. "Do something!"

Cautiously, he approached the tall column of wood. Then, as James reached out for a bottom block, he tripped and knocked the entire tower over. The others gasped.

"You did that on purpose!" Iggy shouted.

"Prove it!" James shouted, looking pleased with himself.

Soon Jenga pieces were being tossed around the room, and suddenly Theo playfully tackled James, who had tackled Iggy. Phil and Olive held Iggy back as she threw empty threats at James while laughing nonstop.

It was total chaos, and Olive loved it.

12.
NOCK

Olive's first weekend at RASCH was like living a dream—
the good kind, not the nightmare kind where she was on
a trapeze with no one to catch her. Upon discovering that
Olive had accidentally brought her mother's clothes instead
of her own, Iggy decided that the whole pod would spend
their Saturday shopping in San Francisco.

Yash ferried them across the bay on BoBu, and Olive was
thrilled by the number of vintage stores that dotted the city.
Though everyone had strong suggestions about what she
should wear, in the end Olive listened to herself and came
away with several retro outfits, plus a coveted pair of clunky
black boots.

When Iggy and James argued over what to do next, it
was Phil who suggested ice cream, and no one had a problem
with that.

"Look!" Theo pointed at one of San Francisco's famous

cable cars. "That'll take us to Ghirardelli Square. They have the best hot fudge sundaes!" Olive and the others raced to board the trolley. It was crowded, so they had to stand, but none of them seemed to mind. As the cable car traversed up and over the hills of San Francisco, for the first time ever Olive felt like she was actually making friends. She hadn't been this happy since she last saw Mimi.

On Monday morning, pod 101 was all business. The five of them sat quietly waiting. Waiting for what—no one was sure. They had spent most of the weekend trying to guess why they had been selected and for what, but no one had a clue.

Olive opened her notebook to a blank page and looked up at Monica, who was writing on the whiteboard with surprisingly delicate handwriting, all swoops and swirls.

"What is"—Olive craned her head to read—"NOCK?"

"*We* are a division of NOCK," Modest said from the back of the classroom.

"Knock?" Iggy looked confused.

"*NOCK,*" Modest repeated.

"Who's there?" Theo asked.

It was Phil who sorted it out. "You're telling us that the name of this 'elite force' is NOCK?"

"Correct!" Modest did a little jig, the kind where his upper body remained stationary but his legs moved at an alarmingly rapid rate.

"*NOCK* stands for 'No One Can Know,'" Monica said, adding this on the board. "In fact, we are so undercover that even other entities within NOCK don't know about us. Our mission includes ensuring the safety of the community, guarding the possessions of the citizens, and preventing civil disorder."

Olive's breath hitched in excitement. They had a mission! A purpose! Her pen flew across her paper as she attempted to write this all down.

Phil looked up from her rings. "I can't find anything on NOCK online."

Monica nodded. "We are a hundred percent under the radar. In the past, NOCK operatives have guarded public figures, rescued citizens, retrieved stolen goods, and held bake sales—all without anyone knowing who we are."

James cleaned his glasses and put them back on. His red bow tie was crooked. "So, is this a government-sanctioned entity like the CIA, FBI, NSA? Or are we rogue?"

"Rogue, I hope!" Iggy said, grinning slyly. Olive found herself grinning, too.

"We are somewhat government-sanctioned." Monica sounded vague. "Though the head of NOCK is Anonymous."

"You mean no one knows who they are?" Theo sounded impressed.

"That, and their code name is 'Anonymous,'" Modest clarified. "Only a few select people know their true identity. Other high-ranking officials give us our assignments. At times we may even go off the grid for the good of the mission."

Phil raised her hand. "So, are we, like, junior police? Or spies?"

"No," Monica replied. "As youth operatives, you will go where the police cannot. As a team, we prevent chaos and catch lawbreakers, but we don't pass information back and forth. Not spies."

"Not spies," Modest reiterated firmly.

Monica gave him a sweet smile. "Prior to our marriage, Modest was a spy. He didn't like it."

"Too many double and triple agents," he confessed. "Very confusing."

"Are we superheroes?" Theo stuck his arms out like he was flying. "Do we get to wear costumes? I have my own cape!"

"We're not about standing out. We're about blending in," Modest clarified. Olive found this ironic since he was wearing a turquoise jumpsuit and matching ballet slippers.

Monica LaMonica crossed her strong arms. "As undercover operatives, we work both outside of the law and within to protect the citizenry. We only take on cases where someone has been wronged or is in danger—and we aim to correct that." When she scrutinized the five recruits, everyone sat up a bit straighter. "In the past, NOCK was primarily made up of adults. But those operatives are too easy to trace, given their ages and life history."

Olive wondered if this was why her social media and library fines had disappeared. Had she been considered for NOCK even before she'd arrived at RASCH? Were her parents in on this? Then she briefly imagined her mother off in some distant land with her orange suitcase, buying yet another snow globe to bring home.

Olive shook her head. There was no way her parents knew. She hadn't even heard from her mother about their swapped suitcases. But then, why should this be any different from all their other business trips? A dull ache thudded in Olive's chest, but she pushed it away and focused on her notes.

Modest glided around the room. "We need operatives with fresh eyes, fresh thinking, who aren't afraid to try new things. Plus, given your age, no one would ever suspect you when you're on a mission."

As the magnitude of what was happening set in, Olive's breaths became short and quick. It was like Christmas morning when she was little and saw that Santa had visited in the night. Meanwhile, Phil was perfectly still as if soaking it all in. Iggy could not stop fidgeting, and Theo, who was normally laid-back, was leaning so far forward in his chair he risked falling. Only James looked suspicious.

"Each of you has special skills, most of which you aren't even aware of yet," Monica informed the group. "You will undergo intensive training. Afterward, if you're still here—you'll be given an assignment of dire consequence."

The more Olive heard, the more uncertain she became. She wasn't sure if she was undercover operative material. "Have you done this before?" she asked. "You know, with kids?"

"We tried it with teens." Modest wedged a window open, just as the sun shone on the Golden Gate Bridge in the distance. When he turned around, his features were etched with regret. "It didn't work."

"They all perished. Tragic deaths. Sad parents. Lawsuits." Monica's words were met with stunned silence. Ignoring the horrified looks on the students' faces, she shouted, "Joking! We discovered that teens stand out far more than they blend in. They complain a lot, court high drama, and, of course, there's their attitudes." Monica quickly became serious. "We have high expectations for this pod, but this information absolutely cannot be shared with anyone else. Is that understood?"

The recruits nodded. Olive and Phil exchanged nervous glances. Monica continued, satisfied. "For generations, a select part of RASCH has been an elite training facility to identify up-and-coming crime fighters, law enforcement operatives, detectives, and support staff. Some of the instructors here are NOCK, but most are not. We don't even know who our own peers are. Our freestanding unit"—she gestured to the class—"will all be mixed in with the general populace of students, educators, and others who have zero clue that RASCH is anything but a creative arts academy. And it is to remain as such! Our cover *cannot* be broken. To do so could endanger the entire operation."

Modest looked delighted, adding, "You five are the youngest NOCK operatives ever! It took a lot of convincing to get Anonymous to approve."

"Pod 101 is an experiment," Monica conceded. "But an important one, a program we've needed for a long time. Your distinct skills complement each other. This, coupled with your age, is our biggest advantage. It's often the underdogs who are in the position to make the most dramatic differences."

Olive had never been picked for anything, much less for an "elite force of specially trained operatives." She could feel her face flush when she admitted, "I was scared during a lot of the splores. I didn't know what I was doing half the time."

Phil nodded in agreement. "Me too."

"That's a plus!" Monica declared, startling them both. "Admitting you don't know something is a rare asset."

Modest jumped in. "Fear is a great asset, too. It keeps you fresh and on your toes. The bravest, most confident people I know still have fears. Every successful NOCK agent has a good dose of fear in them!"

Olive allowed herself to be slightly reassured. *At least,* she thought, *if not knowing what's going on and fear are good things, then I should be great at this.*

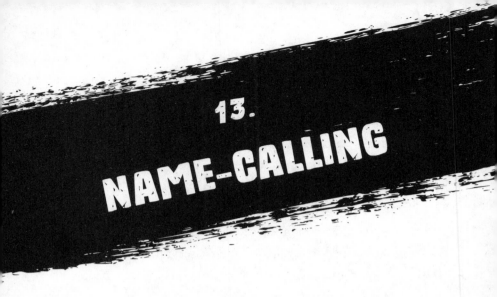

13.
NAME-CALLING

At lunch, NOCK's newest recruits tried not to draw attention to themselves—not that anyone ever noticed them, anyway. It was mind-boggling trying to absorb all the information that had been thrown their way. Theo was having trouble even completing his sentences, and Olive kept pinching herself to make sure she wasn't dreaming.

Their first mission was to come up with a code name for their group. Several ideas were batted around, like Enforcers, Juvenile Justice, and Legends.

"I don't know," Olive finally said after about the hundredth suggestion. She pushed her peas to the other side of the plate with her fork. "They all sound pretty serious when, really, we're just a bunch of misfits."

Iggy cried, "That's it!"

"It's perfect," Theo agreed, looking at Olive in awe. "It's us."

"What? Misfits?" Olive shook her head. "I wasn't suggesting that it be—"

"It's solid," James thought out loud. "A misfit is a person who is different from other people, and who does not seem to belong in a particular group or situation."

"I nominate the Misfits as our code name." Phil raised her fork in the air.

"Second it," James quickly agreed.

"Okay, it's official. We are the Misfits!" Iggy declared.

Everyone paused to enjoy the moment. They were no longer just some random kids. They were all Misfits of NOCK.

After lunch, training began in earnest when the Misfits were greeted by Modest and Monica near the entrance of their wing.

"Before you can be entrusted with a mission, you have to *earn* your NOCK status." Monica's gaze locked on Olive, who immediately pulled her shoulders back.

"Good posture is key to good balance," Mimi had always told her. And Olive already knew that being a Misfit would be a balancing act.

"We have been evaluating your evolving skills, but you must be ready to work as a cohesive team. Part of the reason you five were selected was that your talents and personalities balance each other's."

Balance. There was that word again.

The Misfits nodded with various degrees of confidence, with Iggy on one end and James on the other. Olive herself was a little nervous, but she couldn't wait to get started. Other than the Misfits, the only group she had ever belonged to was the Chess Club. But when the other two members quit, there was no point in her staying in it alone.

"Training is essential." Modest lifted a leg over his head with ease. *Is he even aware that he's always doing ballet moves?* Olive wondered. "Follow me!"

The Misfits racewalked as they wove through several unassuming side doors and through an endless hallway. At last, they stopped in front of a delicate oil painting of an adolescent Gloria Vanderwisp, awash in so many layers of chiffon that she resembled a wedding cake. On her lap was a black cat with distinctive green eyes.

"Dame Gloria loved Winky so much." Modest's voice was soft. "After her cat passed away, her parents had a special piece of jewelry commissioned. She never goes anywhere without wearing her signature Winky pin."

"Rough-cut black diamonds, alexandrite emerald eyes, whiskers forged from single lines of yellow diamonds." Monica sounded unimpressed. "I'm not big on jewelry. Instead, give me a good pair of titanium high-tech night-vision binoculars any day."

Modest glanced around to make sure they hadn't been followed. "The room we are about to enter is exclusively for our NOCK pod and therefore secret from the rest of RASCH. From this moment on, most of our lessons will take place in here, and our physical defense training will be in the gymkhana."

Monica poked the painting of Dame Gloria in

the nose. Silently, a paneled wall slid open to reveal a thick, solid steel door that swung aside with an assertive whoosh.

James was the first in and almost fainted from happiness. As the others entered, a chorus of *ooh*s and *aah*s filled the large space.

The expansive library was lined with books from floor to ceiling. An elaborate antique sword collection was on display by the right-hand wall. Cozy velvet sofas waited near the aisles, and several wooden ladders on wheels were standing by to reach the top shelves. Olive had never seen so many books in her life.

"When Foggy Manor was taken over by the prison system, the warden created the world's largest lawbreaker history library." Modest scampered up and down the ladders, reminding Olive of a hamster, albeit one who was six and a half feet tall.

Monica winked at James, whose mouth was hanging open. "All major and minor crimes of the century are cataloged in here. The library stopped shelving books in 1943, when the prison was shuttered and the island was taken over by an unnamed trust fund. Still, there's plenty here for you to research and to learn from."

"This also doubles as your panic room." Against the far wall at the top of a ladder, Modest opened a hidden door to reveal a pantry stocked with snacks, beverages, board games, and weapons.

"Panic room?" Olive echoed. She suddenly realized that being a NOCK operative could be dangerous—like walking a tightrope. A shiver of excitement ran through her.

"A panic room is a secret bunker designed to be invulnerable to attack or intrusion," James piped up from behind a stack of books in his arms. "The White House has one, and so do lots of multimillionaires' homes."

By the entrance, Monica flipped a switch on the wall that said EMERGENCY. Another bookcase slid open to reveal a room crammed with computers, tools, and high-tech equipment. "Philomena, will this do for your workshop?"

Speechless, Phil walked toward it like someone in a trance. Olive couldn't help smiling.

Theo was appraising the battle scene painted on the ceiling, which depicted knights facing off against a large dragon. It looked like the dragon was winning. "So what's this place called?" Theo wondered out loud. "We can't exactly say 'Let's head to the panic room' without it sounding suspicious."

"Laundry Room!" Iggy shouted. She was holding an antique sword in each hand.

"Laundry Room?" Olive asked.

"No one wants to be caught in a place full of stinky, dirty laundry," Iggy answered matter-of-factly, swinging the swords over her head.

She did have an excellent point.

"Okay! Now that we have that settled, let's get to work. Iggy, put the weapons away," Monica said sternly. "Crime, chaos, and natural disasters do not take time off, and neither should we. An ancient obelisk has gone missing from the Karbon Art Museum, a prolific jewel thief is on a robbery spree, and there's a crack in the Oroville Dam that could flood Northern California. The sooner you're up to speed, the faster we can get you in the field."

Everyone settled onto the sofas and quickly became focused. Their first Laundry Room session was in language arts, where they were assigned to write a paper using someone else's identity.

Some of the Misfits hesitated, but Olive finished her paper in record time. She and Mimi used to play a game called Wait! Who's That? where they'd point out a stranger and make up a story about them.

Olive noticed that each of their lessons seemed to play to a different Misfit's strengths. Anything having to do with computers and tech was Phil's domain. In physics and math, Iggy was stunningly skilled at gauging distance (down to the inch) and calculating the speeds of cars, bullets, and rockets. Theo had an endless fascination with geography and natural disasters. And despite being the youngest Misfit, James had a nearly encyclopedic knowledge of history and obscure facts, making him an invaluable team member at Trivial Pursuit.

Once their lessons finished, it was afternoon snack time. As they munched on Gala apples, nuts, and cheese, Modest and Monica took a short coffee break in their faculty lounge, whose door was hidden behind a huge tapestry of goats frolicking over a bridge. Inside, the small room was crammed with computers, two matching recliners held together with duct tape, and a loud espresso machine.

Olive was both tired and energized at the same time. "Me

too!" Phil admitted as they watched James eat the last of the Brie.

"Now that we've completed our Laundry Room sessions for today, let's head to the gymkhana!" Modest exclaimed, leaping out of the faculty lounge and landing on pointe.

"He had too much caffeine again," Monica explained. "It happens."

"Who wants to learn how to fight?" Modest shouted.

Monica raised her hand, and both she and Modest began to laugh.

Olive quickly sat up, her tiredness replaced by excitement.

"One never knows when a sidewinder kick or a reverse second-position punch could thwart a felony," Modest continued, "or stop a criminal confrontation, or save the day. . . ."

Iggy was already at the door while he was still talking, with the rest of the Misfits close behind.

14.
MISFITS

Given the right circumstances, time could really fly. That's how Mimi's acrobatics students always felt when learning the Three Ts—trapeze, tightrope, and tumbling. Olive began training when she was a toddler. After lessons, she used to unwind in Mimi's festive living room, surrounded by her collection of ceramic mice. Her favorite was always the tiny mouse with a feather pen.

"I wonder what she's writing," Olive had said on her last visit.

Mimi kissed the top of her only grandchild's head. "She's writing, 'I love you. I miss you. I will see you again soon.'"

Olive ran her finger over the tiny chip on the mouse's ear. "She's broken."

"She's not broken—she's unique! That chip makes her more interesting, don't you think?" Mimi rolled up a sleeve

and pointed proudly to a long scar on her arm. "Perfection is boring. Flaws are interesting."

Back in Foggy Manor, the gymkhana had been transformed into an elaborate training room, complete with rows of weights, a spiral slide, boxing equipment, and a nice assortment of weapons. Mirrors lined the walls, along with six portable ballet bars of various heights.

One for each Misfit, and one for the ballet master.

Modest extended his arms wide and welcoming, then bowed so deeply that his head dusted the floor. "Misfits," he began with a flourish, "*this* is where you'll learn ballet!"

Ballet?! Olive's heart lifted. Mimi used to take her to see the *Nutcracker* ballet every winter. When she was little, Olive had always wanted to be the Sugar Plum Fairy.

Theo's curls flopped from side to side as he shook his head. "Ballet? No. No one said we had to do ballet. I can't dance. I'm too awkward!"

"It's true," Iggy agreed. "Just look at him."

But Monica's eyes were locked on the giant TV in the corner of the room, where the news was warning viewers of the master jewel thief yet again.

"During his latest robbery at a private penthouse party, not only did the thief take all the jewelry, but he also left something behind," the anchor intoned. The camera cut to a gold crown embossed on a black calling card. *"Based on this, I think it's fair to call him . . . the Bling King!"*

Olive squinted at the image. It almost looked familiar, but she couldn't quite place why.

"Gotta keep an eye out for that one," Monica warned. When a commercial for KittyKon, a cat convention, came on, she hit mute. "Now, Modest will teach you ballet and other fitness moves, while I will teach boxing, mixed martial arts, and an assortment of fighting techniques. Like us, all these moves work in concert. Each skill requires strength and stamina, and combined they provide fluidity, grace, and the element of surprise." She winked at Iggy. "You will also have weapons training."

Iggy let loose a "Huzzah!"

"But dance and movement class first! Hurry, hurry!" Modest instructed the Misfits to stand in the middle of the room, and they quickly obeyed. "Six feet apart, please." Holding a bicycle horn high, Modest said, "When you hear the honk, I want you to fall gracefully."

Phil whispered to Olive, "Did I hear him correctly?"

"And . . . *now!*" The horn blasted.

Everyone sat on the floor.

"No, no, no, no, no!" Monica scolded. "Modest said to fall, not to have a picnic."

"Again!" Modest blasted the horn.

For the next three hours, the Misfits practiced falling. It was harder—and more painful—than it looked.

"Drop and roll! Drop and roll!" Modest thundered. "Give into the fall. You control it. Don't let it be the boss of you."

"Phil, tuck in your chin!"

"Olive, throw your arm up—better to land on an arm than your noggin!"

"James, loosen up! Roll your body to the side!"

"Theo, bend those wrists, elbows, and knees! You look like a plank."

"Iggy, you got this!"

By the end of the lesson, they were exhausted. Modest was particularly tired. He had yelled so much that he was in desperate need of a cup of honey lemon tea.

"Falling correctly is the first step in stellar self-defense," Monica told the team as she threw bottles of water at them. All successfully batted them away. "Those were for you to drink," Monica explained as the Misfits chased after the bottles now rolling across the floor. "Always stay hydrated. As for the falling, done correctly, it helps prevent injury and puts your attackers off guard. Observe."

On cue, Modest bolted from his chair and swung at Monica. When his punch started to land, she rolled with it, fell to the ground, and jumped up. "The danger lessens if you know how to react properly."

The Misfits gasped when Monica hit Modest hard. He whirled around in the direction of the punch but remained standing, then swung at Monica.

"Don't ever get too comfortable," Monica cautioned, ducking to avoid his fist. "Remember: tumble, tuck, rock, and roll. Tomorrow, we'll learn to crawl, plus some basic ballet, boxing steps, and what to do if you are punched in the gut or attacked from behind."

In a raspy voice, Modest informed the Misfits,

"While you're here, you will learn confidence, speed, unity, strength, creativity, endurance, and smarts. Take the first letter from each of those words, rearrange them, and what does it spell?"

The room went quiet until Olive stood and yelled, "Success!"

"Correct!" Monica pointed to her as if she had won a game show.

Theo led the applause. Olive blushed. Then the Misfits stumbled back to their rooms, falling down on purpose now and then, to get ready for dinner.

15.

NOSES

Olive's first month at RASCH zipped by quickly with classes in the Laundry Room, exhausting training sessions in the gymkhana, and day trips into San Francisco followed by rousing game nights with her fellow Misfits on the weekends. It wasn't too long before she began to feel like a longtime RASCHer and found herself practicing dance and gymnastics on the front lawn during her breaks, like she truly belonged.

One afternoon, while doing cartwheels past an art pod whose members were painting each other (quite literally), Olive observed Sunny and Yash strolling by, looking more serious than usual. Sunny seemed so distracted that she kept wandering off the path, and even walked smack into a lion topiary that Brood was trimming from atop a wobbly ladder.

"When Dame Gloria sends the next check, we can cover most of the bills," Yash said as she helped Brood up, then skillfully guided her boss back onto the cobblestone walkway.

"Which is why the gala *must* be a success!" Sunny insisted. "Ninety percent of our funds are raised on that one night alone. Plus, there are some rumblings that Dame Gloria may not show up because the Bling King is still at large."

"Well, she wouldn't be a target if she didn't always wear so much jewelry," Yash quickly pointed out. "She looks like a treasure chest with toothpick legs."

Perking up at the mention of Dame Gloria, Olive longed to see this reclusive legendary lady in person. After finishing her cartwheels with a roundoff back handspring, she pretended to tie her shoe as she eavesdropped.

"Our esteemed benefactor is the face of RASCH!" Sunny veered off the path again and headed toward the moat. Yash waited, as if considering her choices, before finally stopping her boss from falling in at the last second. "If Dame Gloria Vanderwisp bails on us, then the remaining patrons will follow suit, and our decades-old allegiance will be kaput!"

Olive glanced at the clock on top of the manor entrance. Unfortunately, she was due in the gymkhana soon. Modest and Monica had wanted to show her something today, so Olive really couldn't be late. A new ballet or boxing move, perhaps? She was getting good at both.

Thoughts of Dame Gloria and the Bling King whirled

around as Olive headed to Foggy Manor. With all the concerns, she was beginning to think that the Misfits might somehow be involved with the two. . . . Her suspicions, however, got sidetracked the moment Olive walked into the gymkhana.

A tightrope that hadn't been there before crossed the entire length of the room, and a trapeze hung from the top of the window, to swing outside and over the courtyard.

"For me?" Olive could barely speak, she was so overwhelmed.

"You said this would help your training." Monica looked pleased. Anything the Misfits needed, NOCK made sure they got. So far, they'd received tech supplies for Phil, even more books for James, yoga equipment for Theo, and a mixed martial arts training robot for Iggy.

Olive had mastered the tightrope almost as soon as she could walk. "Look ahead, not down," she remembered Mimi instructing in her soothing voice. "Take it one step at a time. Do that, and you can go anywhere."

Olive had to wait until she was seven to learn the trapeze. Mimi would hang upside down by her knees, swinging back and forth, while Olive perched on the platform, getting a grip on the trapeze bar. When ready, she'd fly through the air, hook her legs over the bar, and, with her arms stretched out, trust that she'd be caught in her grandmother's capable hands.

Now when Olive mastered a difficult move, it was Modest, Monica, and her fellow Misfits who cheered her on. She was there for them as well, yelling words of encouragement. Olive recalled Primrose and the twins trying to push the Misfits down during the Gymkhana Splore. Here, the Misfits helped each other up.

For the most part, the Misfits worked exceedingly well as a team. James was book smart and cautious. Phil was innovative and insecure. Iggy was strong and headstrong. Theo was charismatic and laid-back.

And Olive . . . sure, Olive was agile, but she was still a little anxious. It was clear why the others had been selected for NOCK, but what exactly did she have to offer? Quietly, she'd begun to wonder: What if *she* let NOCK down? What if she was the weak link on the team?

As she hopped across the tightrope on one leg, bits and pieces of Sunny's conversation began to surface as she continued thinking. The Misfits were a grand NOCK experiment, and RASCH was their base. But if the gala didn't bring in enough funds, then there might be no more RASCH, which meant there would be no more NOCK.

No more NOCK meant no more Misfits, and no more Misfits meant that Olive would be alone once more.

At the end of the tightrope, she pivoted, then hopped back on the other leg as James and Phil threw balls at her. "Harder," Monica ordered. "Try to knock her off!"

Olive gulped but stood a little straighter. She wasn't about to lose her balance, or fail NOCK.

"Don't rush," Monica reminded her. "Pace yourself. Most people lose a battle because they're tired."

The rest of the afternoon, Olive trained harder than ever. When it was time for their last lesson of the day, Modest shoved his finger up his nose. "Now you all do it," he instructed.

Phil was reluctant, but instantly, James had a finger in each nostril. "Does this count for extra credit?" he asked.

As the rest of the Misfits plugged up their noses, Modest explained. "Chances are you will be tailing someone, somewhere, at some time. Most likely you'll be ignored, since you are kids, but we want to give you tools, just in case you're seen."

This, Olive already knew. Few adults paid attention to children. Looking around at her teammates, she knew they all had trouble even getting their own parents to pay attention to them. Theo lamented that unless his dad's assistant reminded him when his birthday was, his father would forget. Phil's parents checked in on a regular basis, but

only to ask about her grades. Iggy's mom was in prison, so she hardly got to see her. And parents were one of the few topics James wouldn't discuss.

"If the person you're tailing suspects you're following them"—Modest pivoted on pointe and stared at Phil, who immediately stiffened—"they're bound to turn around and

look at you. That's when you put your finger in your nose. No one wants to watch someone pick their nose."

The Misfits laughed and practiced until Monica signaled the end and brought out the hand sanitizer.

"When will we get our first assignment?" Iggy asked as Modest used an entire bottle on his huge hands. It was her favorite question.

"When you are ready," Monica LaMonica said brusquely. "We're hoping that will be soon, because there's something brewing and it's about to bubble over."

Olive wondered what it could be. The museum's missing artifacts? The Bling King? An earthquake? A national internet crash?

Whatever it was, Olive hoped that she and the other Misfits would be ready for it soon. All they did was train and train—but for what? Olive was starting to itch for a chance to show that she had what it took to be a Misfit.

16.
SPLISH-SPLASH SPLORE

The next morning, the Misfits were greeted in the gymkhana by Modest Cusak, who was wearing an old-fashioned one-piece striped bathing suit with a brown belt around his waist.

"Today is the Splish-Splash Splore!" He waved a pair of goggles over his head like a lasso.

Monica motioned out the window to the ocean. "Swimming in a pool is one thing, but swimming in the murky, choppy water of San Francisco Bay is another. And as part of the last steps in your training, you will learn how to swim in its unpredictable and unforgiving waters."

Olive had trouble comprehending. Was *swimming* a NOCK requirement?

She'd had issues with swimming since she was five, when her family was on vacation. Despite the tropical scenery, her parents were on their phones most of the time. The sun was warm, the sand white and soft. Glistening water beckoned.

Without warning, little Olive ran giggling into the warm ocean.

She shuddered at the memory. Olive could still remember the way the huge wave had knocked her over and how she'd begun tumbling under the sea.

It had felt like a lifetime of choking on salt water, and Olive could feel her eyes watering even now. Her family had avoided beaches ever since, and her father, Dr. Zang Cobin, used the "incident" as an excuse to never go on vacation again.

Not that any of this stopped the Misfits from marching out to the dock in their swimwear. Olive started to explain that she didn't have a swimsuit, but Monica tossed her a brand-new one-piece.

Now that she was up close to the water's edge, the San Francisco Bay looked even more unforgiving. Olive's insides pitched and plunged. "I can't swim," she finally confessed weakly.

Modest knelt so he could look her directly in the eye. "We know," he said kindly. He handed her a pink floppy plastic something. "Here, blow this up."

As Olive blew and blew, a giant flamingo float began to take shape. When at last the flamingo was seaworthy, Modest yelled, holding his nose, "Follow me one at a time!"

Splash! Modest was in the water.

Splash! Monica was in the water.

Splash! Iggy was in the water.

Splash! Theo was in the water.

Splash! Phil was in the water.

Splash! James was in the water.

Only Olive remained dry, feebly clutching the flamingo, which started deflating when the plug popped out. Frozen on the dock, she stared at the other Misfits. An hour later, when they emerged from the sea soaking wet, laughing and spitting up briny water, shame washed over Olive.

Monica LaMonica observed the only dry Misfit but said nothing. Nor did Modest or any of Olive's new friends. It

was as if she were invisible, just when Olive had thought she was being seen for the first time.

The sun had begun to set by the time the Splish-Splash Splore concluded. Gleefully, Theo led the way as they pirouetted to the dorms to change into dry clothes. Only Olive remained sitting at the dock, still unable to move, until she heard footsteps nearing.

"Nice day, don't you think?" It was Zeke, whose bravery and overconfidence—and lack of fear—had disqualified him from being a Misfit. He considered Olive for a moment. "You okay?"

Olive swallowed. In the presence of Zeke and his dimples, she forgot how to formulate a sentence. "Swim. Cannot do."

Zeke sat down on the low wall that separated the ocean from the island. "Are you liking RASCH?"

Olive kept her eyes out on the bay to avoid looking at him and saying something stupid again. The sunset glowed a comforting orange over the water.

"I love it here," Olive said, realizing that that was true.

"Me too." Zeke sounded a bit melancholy. "Members of my family have been coming to Foggy Island for generations. They really try to be accepting of everyone at RASCH."

Olive faced him. "What do you mean?"

Zeke shrugged. "You know, like if you don't have money or the right background, or even if you don't have parents."

Olive waited for him to continue. "My grandparents

met here when they were both scholarship students. I'm one, too. Most of the students here are." Olive didn't know that. "There are a lot of foster kids, too."

"Foster kids?"

"Yeah, you know. Kids in foster care. Sunny opens her arms to everyone who needs a home and encourages skills people didn't even know they had. There's so much talent at RASCH."

Olive nearly scoffed. She sure didn't feel talented. After this afternoon, she just felt like a fake. "I can't swim," Olive heard herself confessing.

Zeke raised a hand to his eyes. They were green with flecks of golden brown. "I've seen you do backflips across the lawn. You're an amazing acrobat, Olive. Maybe if you just think of swimming like acrobatics under the water, that might help."

Olive let out a nervous laugh. Yet despite this, she was feeling a little better.

"Thanks, Zeke," she said shyly. Then she sighed. Olive couldn't put off facing her teammates forever. She stood up, her knees stiff after sitting so long, and started heading back to the manor. "I'll see you around?"

Zeke waved a friendly goodbye as Olive walked, slowly but determinedly, toward the dining hall. *I can do this,* she thought firmly. After all, if she had any chance of earning her spot as a Misfit, she had to start facing her fears head-on.

17.
COMCHOM

By the time Olive reached the dining hall, dinner was in full swing. The air was thick with conversation, clattering dishware, and the mouthwatering aroma of food. Tonight, more pasta dishes were on the menu, and the dining hall had run out of Butter Bakery rolls.

The Misfits were at their usual table tucked near the back. Iggy and James were sword-fighting with spoons. Theo was leaning over, talking to a boy from another pod, and Phil was scanning the room. When she saw what she was looking for, Phil waved to Olive.

"Where were you?"

"Nowhere," Olive answered vaguely as she put her tray on the table.

"Okay." Phil offered Olive a comforting nod. "I'll give you some space. But if you want to talk, I'm always here."

Olive replied with a hesitant smile. She poked at her

noodles as Phil turned back to the other Misfits, who were now discussing the Bling King. Second-guessing the master jewel thief had become more and more popular and had been dominating the news. In the past week, he had hit three places: a jewelry emporium, a luxury yacht, and the most impressive (or disturbing, depending on what side of politics you were on) of all, a fundraiser at the mayor's house.

He left his calling card behind each time.

Suffice to say, the Misfits were very absorbed in the recent Bling King rumors. If anyone had noticed that Olive was the only one who hadn't gone swimming, they didn't mention it. Were they just being polite, or were they embarrassed for her? In any case, she was grateful not to be the topic of conversation.

Starting that night, Olive began sneaking out her bedroom window after everyone had gone to sleep. If she was going to prove her worth as a Misfit, there was only one thing to do. Silent as a cat, she shimmied down the rainspout in a flawless move that would have made Mimi proud. If she couldn't swim, Olive could at least double her efforts in fighting, mixed martial arts, sleuthing, and deductive logic, even if it meant working after everyone else was asleep.

Based on how the Misfits' training was ramping up, Olive's extra hours ended up paying off. Shortly after the Splish-Splash Splore, the team was sent across the bay to San Francisco to "case the pier and its vicinity for any suspicious activity," as Monica had instructed.

"The assignment is rather vague," Olive noted as Modest juggled ten-pound weights. "Can you tell us more?" The Misfits had learned that unlike the teachers at their various other schools, their RASCH instructors welcomed questions and discussion.

"Is this some kind of warm-up mission, like a rehearsal for the RASCH gala?" Theo asked.

"What do you think?" Monica tossed the question back to the Misfits. They batted it around before all agreeing that it was a distinct possibility. While they hadn't been officially assigned to the gala, as both RASCH students and NOCK operatives, they were expected to be in attendance one way or another, under various cover stories.

What they hadn't yet discussed was the obvious fact that the gala was going to be a formal event full of wealthy attendees. RASCH's richest patrons were expected to appear in their finest evening clothes. And even though the Bling King was on the rise, Olive just knew that it wouldn't stop the socialites from flaunting their jewels. She recalled Sunny and Yash discussing how the future of RASCH depended on the fundraiser—and her stomach flipped at the thought of it being a failure.

"Aren't we supposed to help stop threats like the Bling King?" Phil said what they were all thinking. Nervously, she tapped on her rings.

Olive and James both grimaced. Theo looked like he had just bitten into a sour pickle. Only Iggy seemed thrilled by this idea.

Modest took a large gulp from his ever-present water bottle. "You haven't been given an assignment yet. Stopping the Bling King would be tricky even for the most seasoned NOCK operatives." He gave the team a rare serious look. "Right now, we're asking you to be up to speed on current events on Foggy Island and in San Francisco and the rest of the world. Details count. To have knowledge is to have power. If you're always aware of what's happening around you, then you will more easily find the exact place you should be."

Always be aware of what's happening around you, Olive reminded herself later as she climbed back to her room that night. The statement warmed her heart. Mimi used to say that to her, too.

"To help you on your missions, from here on out, we have something for each of you," Modest continued. "Phil, if you would be so kind?"

Phil rose and fidgeted slightly. "I've been asked to create some tools to help stop lawbreakers and scoundrels." She looked at Monica. "Is it okay if I talk about your . . . you know?"

"Oh, oh! Let me tell," Modest begged. He dimmed the lights for maximum storytelling effect and lowered his voice. Everyone had to lean in to listen. "It was the final round of the Women's World Boxing Championships. Biffney Bravo was down for the count . . . three . . . two . . . The buzzer rang! Monica LaMonica was the winner!"

Modest's face darkened at the memory. "But Biffney Bravo didn't play by the rules. When Monica LaMonica removed her headgear and raised her hands in triumph, Biffney sucker punched her, leaving her deaf in her left ear and permanently damaging her right ear!"

Reliving the moment, Monica winced. "My hearing was only so-so even with hearing aids—until Philomena offered to turbo-tech my ear device. Now I can hear better than all of you combined."

Phil brushed aside the compliment and reached into her bag, pulling out what looked like retainers from the dentist. "I've created communication enhancers for us all. They only work when you talk with your jaw shut, so you're going to have to learn how to speak without moving your lips. To activate it, chomp down hard three times.

"I call it a Communication Chomper, or ComChom. The ComChoms come paired with these EarBuzzes." She held up what looked like miniature marshmallows. "We will use them to talk with each other, undetected. They can also change your voice." She paused, visibly chomping three times. When she opened her mouth, her voice sounded exactly like Modest's. *"Look at me carrying two ballerinas!"*

"Whoa!" the real Modest yelped.

Phil's voice returned to normal. "Now, who wants to be fitted first?"

All at once, the Misfits ran forward.

18.
SMOTE

Yash honked the horn. "Hurry!" she yelled. "You're late!"

Since she'd started her late-night training sessions, Olive was oversleeping and missing breakfast more often. But at least she wasn't the last one to board BoBu. Her stomach growled when she spotted Theo running toward the dock, holding a familiar bakery bag.

"I have"—he panted—"Butter Bakery pastries!" He waved his bag around and pulled out a tart. "Auntie Winnie included a lemon meringue tart for you, Yash."

Yash's pause gave him just enough time to join the other Misfits. Now nibbling contentedly on the tart, Yash steered BoBu toward San Francisco.

Olive was still eyeing the bag in Theo's hand. "Are those for us?" she said, hoping. The thought of butter cookies, crusty croissants, and chocolate cupcakes with fondant frosting cheered her immensely.

113

Theo's cheeks were so red from running that she could hardly see his freckles. "Auntie Winnie asked if I'd deliver these to the Bay Area Community Outreach Center. Poppy bakes them for the volunteers."

"What do they do there?" Yash turned toward them, steering BoBu with her elbow as she popped the last of the tart into her mouth.

"All sorts of things." Theo began listing. "Job training and placement, free childcare, a medical clinic . . ."

Olive tuned out the chatter when she realized none of the pastries were for her. She yawned as BoBu sped along in the water, then closed her eyes. She was going to need all the rest she could get.

After they reached land, Iggy asked Yash to drop them off a few blocks from the community center so they could get their daily cardio in. What Iggy *didn't* say to her was that training never ceased when you were in NOCK.

As they engaged in quick lunges and burpees, four teen boys wearing football jackets rumbled toward them. Olive cringed when one boy tore a Peace Corps poster from a storefront and ripped it up. Another boy with a blond buzz cut carved deep scratches into parked cars with his keys. Once they got close enough, Olive could see the name "Smote" embroidered on his jacket.

He sneered at Olive. "Chinatown's that way!" he said, launching into gibberish that was supposed to sound Chinese. Olive buried her anger and ignored him.

Undeterred, Smote pointed to Phil. "What are you hiding under that scarf?"

Phil's eyes widened, her mouth open in shock. "That is so rude!" she said, her voice unsteady.

A slow grin crossed Smote's chiseled face. He was just warming up. Without missing a beat, he asked Theo, "Yo, Freckle-Face, what you got there?" Smote snatched the Butter Bakery bag from him. "It's party time!" he hollered, throwing Poppy's pastries like they were footballs.

James froze when an orange macaron bounced off his forehead. "Please stop," Theo said, picking up James's glasses off the sidewalk and handing them back to him.

"Please stop," Smote mimicked. Then he lunged, promptly putting Theo in a loose headlock.

Iggy stepped forward. "Leave. Him. Alone," she said, so sweetly that the other Misfits shuddered.

Smote chuckled uneasily and cocked his head at Iggy, who was considerably shorter and about five years younger than him. Still, he recoiled when hit by the full force of Iggy's blistering stare. She marched up to him, arms crossed, until she was just inches away from him.

He stared at Iggy. "Who's gonna make me?"

She motioned to the Misfits. "Me and my friends."

The other football players began to laugh.

Iggy winked at Smote, who didn't flinch. "Three . . . ," she started, and Olive smiled. "Two . . ." The Misfits all got into position, shoulders back and knees bent. In the past she would have been scared, but this time Olive felt confident as she looked the bullies in the eye. "One . . . *go!*"

They couldn't say they weren't warned. On Iggy's count, the Misfit team launched themselves at the football players. Smote released Theo, who crumpled slightly before springing up like one of Poppy's sponge cakes.

Soon, cookies, croissants, teens, and Misfits were all being tossed around. Iggy was delighted when her upper jabs were just as effective on the bullies as they had been on punching bags. When a football player barreled toward her, Olive successfully landed a roundhouse jeté kick. Theo knocked one of Smote's friends off his feet with a crouching sideswipe.

But ultimately, it was Phil who faced down Smote. Blocking his path with a steady glare and an even steadier hand, she aimed and then let loose her patented Time-Out String. "No one bullies me or my friends!"

"Hey!" Smote shouted as the strong, gooey string wrapped around him. "What is this? I can't move!"

Phil grinned. While Olive had snuck around outside at night, practicing sleuthing and fight moves, Phil had been in her workshop developing weapons and destructive distractions.

"This is the police!" a deep voice bellowed. "Leave the little kids alone!"

The teens panicked and scrambled to their feet, running away and abandoning their friend. Olive scanned the area for the police officers, only to find Theo looking pleased with himself. He had used his ComChom to change his voice!

"Little kids?!" Iggy asked as she dusted herself off.

Grinning, Theo said modestly, "It worked, didn't it?"

19.
DIM SUM

While Phil was making an anonymous call to the police so they could retrieve Smote, Olive tapped her on the shoulder and pointed to a security camera that was aimed at the parked cars.

Phil nodded. "And be sure to check the security footage from Kim's Fabrics," she added. "You'll find evidence of the perpetrator defacing private property."

"I'm starving," Iggy announced, promptly reminding Olive that she hadn't had breakfast. Who knew that fighting crime could work up such an appetite?

The Misfits continued to the community center, dropped off the bag of Poppy's pastries that had survived, and then took a bus to a dim sum restaurant in Chinatown. As soon as they were seated, Iggy flexed her muscles. "Next up, the Bling King!"

"Stopping a bunch of idiots from scratching cars isn't the

same as capturing a world-renowned jewel thief," Theo noted as he placed a napkin on his lap.

"Party pooper!" Iggy stuck out her tongue at him. Before he could respond, servers wearing crisp white shirts pushed metal carts by their table. The Misfits marveled over the delectable custard tarts, shrimp and pork shu mai, fluffy char siu bao, and other favorites of Olive's.

"Chī hǎo hē hǎo!" a woman said to Olive as she put a plate of sticky rice on their table.

Olive, who resembled the Chinese side of her family, as opposed to her father's Anglo-Saxon lineage, admitted, "Sorry, I only speak English."

To everyone's surprise, Theo spoke up. "Nǐ zuì xǐhuān de cài shì shénme?"

The server smiled broadly at Theo, and they began chatting in Chinese.

"I didn't know you spoke Mandarin," Olive said as the server wheeled her cart away. She was always learning new things about her friends.

Theo had managed to stuff two shu mai into his mouth. He looked like a chipmunk. "I speak several languages."

Apparently, Olive and Iggy were the only ones who couldn't speak any languages other than English. Mimi had encouraged Olive to take Chinese language lessons when she was younger, but she wasn't interested back then. Until recently, Olive had hated school. But Theo could speak Mandarin, Phil could speak some Farsi, and James was fluent in pig Latin.

Iggy poured hot chili sauce over her food. "I

should have punched Smote, right, James?" she said, grinning cheekily. "Oh, wait. You were busy hiding, like some sort of scaredy-cat."

James pushed his chair away from the table and folded his arms. "Eave-lay e-may alone-way!" he replied in pig Latin.

"Defend and dismantle," Theo continued. He was now working through a plate of panfried turnip cakes. "It's not our job to decimate."

"You know who I'd love to decimate?" Iggy asked as she munched on an egg roll. "The Bling King. What about you, James? You up for a real fight? Today was just a warm-up. Or will you freeze up again?"

"Iggy," Theo said softly, "lay off him."

"Whatever! I'm just teasing," she said defensively. "He knows that."

Phil, Iggy, and Theo continued jabbering about what it'd be like to take on the Bling King, and stealing dim sum off each other's plates. Olive joined the fun on occasion, but she couldn't help noticing that one of them wasn't participating.

Throughout lunch, James stayed quietly focused on a row of uneaten dumplings in front of him, and he was uncharacteristically silent for the rest of the afternoon as they practiced tailing people and employing the finger-in-nose distraction when caught.

In the following days, James stopped showing up in the Laundry Room and gymkhana. At mealtimes, he sat alone with his books. And whenever a Misfit looked in his direction, he defiantly stuck a finger up his nose.

Olive was concerned. Sure, Iggy had teased James, but she teased everyone. Would her words have been enough for him to withdraw as much as he had? Monica and Modest didn't even mention his absences. Maybe, Olive surmised, James was as scared of fighting as she was of swimming.

Even though she didn't completely grasp what was going on with him, she could certainly understand the urge to disappear.

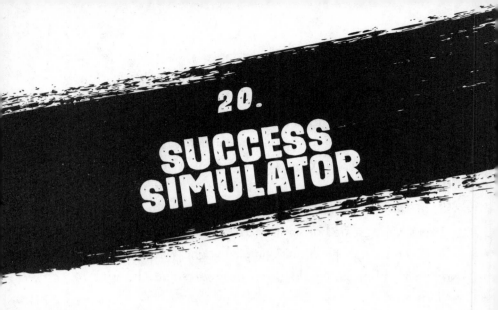

20.
SUCCESS SIMULATOR

As the weeks wore on, the Misfits grew stronger, faster, and more confident. Like professionals, they moved swiftly from lessons in the Laundry Room to physical training in the gymkhana. As a team, they were becoming less clumsy, more cohesive. Olive was sure that if James were there with them, he'd feel the same. "Graceful" would be too strong a word, but still, the team had made amazing progress.

Clearly, Modest and Monica thought so as well. One morning, the Misfits entered the Laundry Room and were met with five colorful kiosks resembling old-fashioned photo booths. Each was labeled with a Misfit's name.

Without waiting for an introduction from Modest and Monica, Olive ran into hers and pulled the curtain shut, darkening the small space. Then there was a bright flash as screens lit up all around her in the booth, glowing blue.

"Olive Cobin Zang, welcome to your SUCCESS Simulator," a soothing woman's voice intoned. "Here, you will be challenged with catastrophes, crimes, natural disasters, and unsolved mysteries, all in the safety of your kiosk." Videos, including a volcano, a sinking ship, a bank robbery, and a black cat, flashed on the screens so quickly that Olive felt dizzy. "In a moment, you will be tasked with resolving a potentially dangerous situation. Using elements of SUCCESS—speed, unity, confidence, creativity, endurance, strength, and smarts—you must come up with a solution using as much time as you need. If you cannot solve the problem, say 'Uncle,' and we will analyze what you have done to date, and go over possible alternatives."

Olive could hardly contain her excitement. Surely this was a test to determine how ready the Misfits were for the field.

"Shall we begin?" the voice crooned.

"Yes!" Olive exclaimed. Instantly, she was launched into her first simulation as the screens cut to a rain forest, the voice describing the situation in the background.

Four hours later, Olive staggered out of her kiosk, feeling light-headed. Theo and Iggy were sprawled across armchairs, looking like they had been through battle.

"I just solved a missing person's case," Olive told them, flopping onto a sofa. "The lawyer had staged her own kidnapping, fled to Costa Rica, and framed her client. I had to climb trees in the rain forest to gather evidence."

"I stopped a volcano from erupting and covering a small

town with lava." Theo's eyes were closed. "A well had to be drilled into the earth and flooded with cold water."

At that moment, Phil pulled aside her kiosk's curtain. "That was *hard*!" she said, adjusting her headscarf. Today's was light blue, matching her dress. "I halted a worldwide cyberattack by using an ancient Egyptian encryption, then created a malware code to stop an army of bots."

When the curtains from the last kiosk were pulled aside, the Misfits stared as James stepped out, looking well rested. "I solved the mystery of D. B. Cooper, the hijacker." He acted as if he had been training with them all week. "I completed my task in an hour, so I went back to do another one."

Before anyone could ask James where he'd been, Monica came striding toward them. "From now on, you will be doing simulations at least twice a day. When warranted, your kiosks will be linked and you may communicate via your ComChoms to work together. Any questions?"

James raised his hand. "Can we do another one right now?"

And so they each completed another simulation, though Olive could barely concentrate on hers. As soon as the second class was over, Iggy made a beeline in James's direction. Olive braced for a fight. Iggy was so unpredictable. And James, Olive knew, was very sensitive. They were like water and oil.

"What?" James eyed Iggy warily. He held a book in front of him like a shield.

Iggy stared hard at him. It was impossible to read her face. After a few seconds that seemed like an hour, she handed

James a stack of papers. "Here's the homework you missed. I made copies."

Theo, Phil, and Olive exhaled. Maybe Iggy couldn't bring herself to apologize for what she'd said, but they all knew that giving James his missing homework assignments was something he appreciated even more.

21.
MEET BEE

Soon enough, the simulations were to become real. Modest and Monica sent the team to San Francisco on an assignment, where they were instructed to follow Phil on where to be debriefed.

Olive had complete and utter trust in Phil. Just yesterday, the two had been sparring, and she'd absolutely loved it. Though Phil had pummeled her, years of acrobatic training had made Olive agile and more athletic than she realized, and she'd fought back, taking control of the match. Phil wasn't as quick as Olive, but her form was excellent. When the bell in the boxing ring rang, the girls took off their headgear, removed their mouth guards, and hugged, pleased at how well matched they were as sparring partners.

Though it went unspoken, the two had become best friends.

After Yash dropped them off in San Francisco, Phil

quickly led them to an empty alleyway and then stopped abruptly, causing Iggy to crash into James, who claimed she'd done it on purpose.

"Stay on the sidewalk," Phil warned. She fiddled with her rings, turning toward the end of the alley, and watched intently as seconds ticked by.

The others glanced at each other, uncertain.

"Just give it another moment . . . ," Phil said apologetically. Suddenly a vehicle rounded the corner, tires screeching, causing them all to jump. The van rumbled down the alley and stopped near them, two wheels on the curb.

"Say hello to Vana," Phil said proudly. "Everyone, hop in!"

"You must be at least eighteen years old to drive with other minors in the car," James said nervously.

"How old are you?" Olive asked.

"I'm almost ten." James lifted his chin in defiance. "I skipped a couple of grades."

Phil waved her hand. "*I'm* not driving," she said, opening the door. "Vana drives herself."

"You built a self-driving car?" Iggy sounded impressed as she walked around the unassuming white van.

"I bought the vehicle used," Phil said modestly. "I merely modified it. Who wants to see the inside?"

As Phil showed off all the features, the team was amazed by every little detail. The interior was now a high-tech security and surveillance dream. Behind the five seats crammed in the front, large screens lined both walls toward the back of the van.

"I can activate the scrambler, so if Vana shows up on security cameras, she looks like a gray station wagon driven by an exhausted mom with two kids," Phil explained. Then she pointed to the biggest computer monitor. "Here we go— meet Bee!"

On the screen, the exterior of Foggy Manor came into view. "We're seeing what Bee sees," Phil said, tapping the rings on her fingers. "Bee is a super-small, super-stealth drone that can track and laser anyone or anything. She even looks like a bee, but she can carry the weight of a small car. Watch. . . ."

Bee buzzed through the mansion and stopped by the entrance to the Laundry Room, where Modest and Monica were waiting. "There you are," Monica said. "Bee is here just in time." On the screen, she led them all into the Laundry

Room, where a safety cable was lowered from the little drone. Modest grabbed it, and as Bee rose, so did he.

"Woo-hoo!" Modest yelped happily from several feet up in the air.

Monica nodded to Bee and acknowledged her. "The annual RASCH gala is approaching fast, and this year's will be the biggest event in the history of the school," she continued without missing a beat as Modest flitted through the air, striking dramatic poses. "It will be honoring Dame Gloria Vanderwisp and the Dame Gloria Vanderwisp Foundation."

Her face darkening, Monica paused. "Despite rumors to the contrary, and threats of a possible Bling King appearance, Dame Gloria has agreed to attend—based on Sunny's guarantee of tight security. Which means big money will be on Foggy Island that evening."

"And where there's money, thieves follow," Modest added, getting serious as Bee lowered him to the ground with a thud.

"I'm going to need to work on that," Phil noted as Modest leaped up.

"*The Bling King,*" Iggy whispered, almost reverently. "On Foggy Island."

"At the same time, Dame Gloria is but one benefactor, and not everyone is so generous," Modest continued, brightening. "Misfits, your mission today is reconnaissance! We've caught wind of a secret meeting at Le Pas de Chat Café this afternoon, where some of the school's biggest patrons plan to discuss whether they will continue funding our illustrious RASCH. Woe be the day if they cease donating." He wiped a tear from his eye. "Your mission is to infiltrate their meeting and gather information on what their next steps will be."

"Any questions?" Monica asked. The Misfits shook their heads. "Then we await your report. Oof!"

"Oof! Oof! Oof!" the team replied, and Phil disconnected from Bee. They were quiet for a moment.

"I didn't realize things were that bad," James said, buckling his seat belt.

Olive admired Vana's tinted windows. They could see out, but no one could see in. "Yeah, things are kinda dire," she told him. It seemed Sunny and Yash had reason to be concerned, all those weeks ago. A deep feeling of unease revisited Olive. "If the money dries up, then the school shuts down."

"No way are we gonna let that happen," Iggy insisted. She turned to Phil. "Can I sit in the driver's seat?"

Phil shook her head. "No. Only me. Everyone, Com-Choms activated?"

"Affirmative," they all answered. And with that, Vana hit the road and headed toward Le Pas de Chat Café.

When they arrived, it quickly became clear that the restaurant was super fancy. Sports cars lined up outside for valet parking, and there was a greeter wearing white gloves at the door. Vana parked across the street, where Iggy and James would monitor which benefactors were arriving, while Phil kept tabs on all their technology.

To blend in with the restaurant clientele, Olive and Theo changed into a couple of plain, boring suits among the supplies in the van. One whole Misfit training session had been disguises. Olive took a deep breath as she checked her unassuming reflection in the mirror. Then she and Theo walked casually into the restaurant—and were quickly stopped by the stuffy maître d'.

"Pardon!" His accent was French. Olive froze. So soon into their first mission, and they were caught already?!

To her astonishment, Theo shook the man's hand and began to converse with him in flawless French. When Theo pointed to Olive, they both doubled over with laughter.

"Merci beaucoup!" Theo told the maître d'. "Come on, Olive!" He smiled widely as he all but dragged Olive into the restaurant. There was so much she didn't know about the other Misfits!

It was after lunch hour, and the restaurant wasn't crowded. They found seats in a quiet corner and moved a couple of tall potted plants between them and the rest of the tables.

"There!" Olive motioned discreetly. At a table near the center of the room, she recognized six patrons from their Foggy Manor portraits. Hidden by the plants, the two Misfits adjusted their EarBuzzes and listened in.

"RASCH has lost its luster. . . ."

"But . . . Dame Gloria doesn't back failures."

"Dame Gloria hasn't gotten her gems stolen. I *have*," a woman in a mink coat said emphatically. She flung a black calling card onto the table.

"If Gloria Vanderwisp continues to donate to RASCH, I will, too. I can't afford to be snubbed by her," said a man in an impeccably tailored suit as he piled caviar onto a tiny piece of toast.

"RASCH is past its prime." Another lady in a designer dress cut up her steak and fed it to the teacup poodle cradled in her lap. "Nothing ever happens there. Why keep donating to an outdated institution?"

"Well, I'm boycotting the gala. The last person I want to see is the Bling King."

Olive chomped three times and whispered to the other Misfits through her ComChom, "It seems like half are going to the gala and half are boycotting. If Dame Gloria bails, then they all will—"

Olive's report was interrupted by a message from Foggy Island. Through their EarBuzzes, Modest sounded like he was right there with them. "Misfits"—he was out of breath— "we have a Code Bagel! Make your way to Pier 45 immediately. There's an emergency, and you're the closest team!"

"We're on it!" Phil assured Modest, her voice a little shaky.

Olive's heart skipped a beat. She and Theo gave each other the slightest of nods. Then, in unison, they stood up from their table, left Le Pas de Chat Café, and hopped into Vana across the street.

22.
CODE BAGEL

"A Code Bagel?" James sounded confused as he buckled up. "I don't remember studying that."

Phil entered the driving coordinates into Vana's directional feed. "Whenever something is 'code,' it means it's top secret."

"Danger lurks," Iggy said excitedly.

Theo had gone white as a sheet, making his freckles stand out more than normal.

"We can do it, whatever it is," Olive said decisively. She wondered if it involved bagels or if Modest just called it that because that's what he'd had for breakfast. "Speed, unity, confidence, endurance, creativity, strength, and smarts spell 'SUCCESS'!" she reminded the team.

While the others nodded, James corrected her. "You got it in the wrong order. You spelled 'SUCECSS.'"

"You guys!" At the back of the van, all the screens were lit up in front of Phil. "Let's leave the spelling for Scrabble later. Monica, I've reprogrammed the traffic signals. We can be on-site in fourteen minutes." Then she informed the Misfits, "The SS *Jeremiah O'Brien* is in trouble."

All watched as a huge ship loomed on one of the screens.

"Who's Jeremiah?" Theo asked. The color was slowly returning to his face.

As Vana started sailing through all the traffic lights, Olive couldn't help but admire Phil, who had programmed them to turn green.

"The SS *Jeremiah O'Brien* is only one of two remaining functional Liberty ships"—James began rattling off statistics, only this time the others were paying close attention to him—"of over twenty-seven hundred that were launched during World War II. These days, the ship takes tourists on daily excursions."

Phil's rings lit up as she accessed the ship's security cameras and broadcast them on the monitors. "I'm sending Bee ahead," she reported. "Wait! She's tracking something under the ocean."

On a small screen, Phil zoomed in on the moving object that Bee was capturing on her camera. Phil swiveled to another image, and immediately, her specialized design program began constructing a prototype of what was beneath the surface.

"That's an old World War II underwater torpedo!" James tried to leap up, but his seat belt held him in. "It's headed toward the *O'Brien*!"

"Looks like that's its target," Phil confirmed. "And it's less than twenty-five miles away."

Monica came on through their EarBuzzes. "We can't involve the military because the government doesn't want an international incident. Misfits, we need you to help avert disaster."

There was electricity in the air as the five let this sink in. They had trained for things like this, but instead of a simulation, it was the real deal.

"Everyone, I'm setting your ComChoms on override," Phil told them. "No need to chomp three times if you want to speak."

Olive hadn't taken her eyes off Bee's screen. The tiny drone was locked on the torpedo, even though it was submerged.

"I'd gauge it to be about sixty-five feet underwater," Iggy calculated. One of her simulators had readied her for this. "It's traveling at forty miles per hour, which makes it about sixteen and two-thirds minutes before impact."

James tugged on his bow tie. "That's slow for a torpedo. Maybe it's designed to destroy but not kill?"

Olive's heart was racing. "We can't take that chance."

23.
SS JEREMIAH O'BRIEN

The SS *Jeremiah O'Brien* was docked at the northernmost point of the city, and by the time Vana pulled up, there was a parade of people boarding the huge ship. They were all wearing purple outfits and red hats, and Olive noticed a sign near the entrance: PRIVATE PARTY: WELCOME RED HAT SOCIETY!

There was no time to waste. While Phil stayed in Vana to track the torpedo, the rest of the team headed out.

"What's the plan?" Iggy asked as the Misfits ran toward the ship.

"Can't we just clear the ship by telling everyone that a torpedo is headed their way?" Olive suggested. All that training had paid off—she wasn't even panting.

"And cause a panic?" James asked pointedly.

"Do you have a better idea?" Iggy sounded cross.

James stopped abruptly, causing the rest of them to pause.

"As a matter of fact, I do," he said, turning and heading back to Vana.

"We've done these a hundred times before." Through their EarBuzzes, everyone could hear James and Phil arguing inside the van. "This *is* Battleship."

"James, this is not a game!" Olive wasn't used to Phil sounding so stern. She smiled a bit, proud that her friend was taking charge. "Just because you've forced us to play Battleship a thousand times doesn't mean it will translate to real life!"

"Girl found her voice," Iggy commented approvingly. She motioned to Olive and Theo. "Let's go. It'll be easier to clear the ship on board than by standing in the parking lot."

"But we're not wearing red hats." Theo motioned to the line of people taking selfies. "We can't just cut in line."

"We can if we want to save lives," Olive assured him. "Follow my lead."

There seemed to be a hundred red hats, and everyone was talking about the same thing. . . .

"If I'm not careful, the Bling King will come for my diamond necklace!"

"He's gotten picky and won't touch anything that's worth under ten million!" said a lady with a kitten peering out of her purse. "Yours is cubic zirconia."

Olive pushed to the front of the line. "Excuse us, we're student volunteers," she explained. "Welcome, everyone!"

Just then, a bell rang, followed by an announcement over the public-address system. "This is Captain Crunch speaking. . . ."

"From the cereal?" Theo asked, surprised.

"Welcome aboard the SS *Jeremiah O'Brien,*" the captain broadcast. "We will be setting sail soon."

"We need Captain Crunch's support to clear the ship," Olive reasoned. In agreement, the Misfits slipped past the front of the line, then separated to find the captain. "You can cover more ground when you split up," Modest had taught them.

As Olive ran down the deck in one direction, she could hear James explaining through her EarBuzz, "In Battleship, you need to distract your enemy—" His voice was now calm and confident, not like the usual James, who tended to overtalk.

"Right! Once I scramble the coordinates," Phil cut in, now following James's logic, "I'll tap into the torpedo's onboard computer and trick it into thinking the battleship—the *O'Brien*—is out at sea."

"Conceal and confuse." There was approval in his voice. "That's always been my strategy."

Olive nodded in agreement. She refocused on her own task, darting through the ship, opening door after door and scanning for anyone who looked like they could be the captain.

"I think I found him," came Theo's voice through the EarBuzz. Olive stopped running through the ship's restaurant. "He's at the helm, but the door is bolted shut from the inside."

"I can break into that," Iggy assured him. "Be right there."

By the time Olive reached the head of the ship,

Iggy was kneeling by the door, pulling what looked like a dental instrument from her pocket. Theo stood on guard nearby, watching for tourists.

Within seconds, the door swung open to reveal a set of stairs. The trio took them two by two to the next floor and found an open room with large windows. In the center of the wheelhouse was a man with a big white mustache, wearing a captain's uniform.

"Hello?" He adjusted his cap. "Sorry, kids, but no tourists are allowed up here."

"You must evacuate the ship now!" Iggy ordered urgently.

The captain had a jolly laugh. "I'm in charge here, not you, young lady."

James came in over their EarBuzzes. "There should be a VHF—very high frequency radio—on the bridge."

"I've just hacked into it and connected it to your Com-Chom," Phil said. "Theo, you're good to go!"

Theo turned away from Captain Crunch and triggered his ComChom voice alteration. "Ahoy, Captain Crunch!" came a call from the helm.

Olive was impressed. Theo sounded like a middle-aged man with a Boston accent.

Captain Crunch waved Iggy away and picked up his radio. "Captain Crunch speaking."

"Sedley Smythe from the Department of Safety here," Theo continued. "We have a nine-one-one, nonsmelly gas leak. You must evacuate everyone on board the *O'Brien*—"

Theo was still talking when Captain Crunch switched to

the loudspeaker. "This is Captain Crunch speaking. Everyone must evacuate the ship immediately. All crew on deck to assist. Repeat, evacuate immediately!" He gave the Misfits a stern look. "Kids, that means you, too!"

Captain Crunch hurried the Misfits down the stairs, then rushed off to join his crew. Olive and the others tried to hurry stragglers along but were met with resistance.

"I have a ticket!" one person insisted, and several nodded, all holding up pieces of paper.

Olive didn't have time for this. She programmed her own ComChom voice changer. When she spoke, the deep voice of Darth Vader echoed around them. "I hereby command you to leave *now*—or else!"

Everyone was quick to scurry after that.

When the last passengers had evacuated, Theo reported to Phil and James through his EarBuzz. "The ship is clear, and we're in the parking lot. How far away is the torpedo?"

"It's still heading straight for the *O'Brien*," came Phil's tight voice.

Olive swallowed nervously and glanced at the ship behind them. Sirens sounded in the distance—emergency vehicles would be arriving soon, and they would be bringing technicians to check the ship for the gas leak. "I've scrambled the torpedo's tracking signal, but I can't disable the projectile," Phil continued. "It will still explode on impact!"

Olive's heart skipped.

"Can you reverse the course of the torpedo's path?" James asked in a rush.

Now Olive's palms were starting to sweat. This was a thousand times more stressful than the SUCCESS simulations.

"I'm trying," Phil said evenly, but a hitch in her voice betrayed her.

"You have five minutes before it hits the *O'Brien,*" James warned. Olive and Iggy held their breath. Theo, who was already a head taller than the others, stood on his tiptoes, watching for the emergency vehicles.

"Okay!" Phil reported. "I've locked into the torpedo's tracking device. And . . . there! I'm creating a ghost ship to trick it into turning around and striking the submarine that initiated the strike."

"Two minutes and counting." If James was nervous, he didn't sound like it.

Olive, Theo, and Iggy joined hands as the emergency vehicles pulled up. Law enforcement started walking toward the ship, ready to put up yellow caution tape at the ship's entrance.

"Five seconds." James continued his countdown. "Four . . . three . . ."

"I've reversed the trajectory!" Phil cried. Iggy gave a loud exhale. "Plus I've sped up the torpedo to strike the submarine. Bee has not detected any sign of life onboard. It's being controlled remotely!"

Olive held her breath.

Boom! Near the horizon over the sea, a tall tower of water shot into the air.

The Misfits were united in stunned silence as the water rained into the ocean. Next to the *O'Brien,* technicians began talking to Captain Crunch as the police eyed the Misfits.

"Kids," a police officer said, coming over to them, "this is not a playground. You need to leave."

The Misfits began walking away slowly. Olive's legs felt weak.

"I'm glad no one was hurt," Theo said, looking somber. The others nodded.

"Mission accomplished," Monica said over their Ear-Buzzes. "Well done, Misfits. It's time to head home."

24.
DECOMPRESSION

After being dropped off with James to meet BoBu, Phil had sent the van to her unmarked garage. "No one needs to know where Vana is parked when we're at RASCH," she had explained. "This guarantees her safety."

Everyone was silent as they piled into BoBu, not that that stopped Yash from trying to make conversation. "There was a big explosion in the water." She was steering through the choppy waves. "It could be seen from all over the city! Anyone know anything about that?"

The Misfits shook their heads and were uncharacteristically quiet all the way back to Foggy Island.

"Interesting," Yash noted wryly. "I would have thought you'd have seen it, too." She didn't try talking to them again after that.

When they reached the safety of the Laundry Room, a

large assortment of ship-shaped cookies was awaiting them. There were even cookies with Captain Crunch's face on them.

"We had Poppy make these special for you completing your assignment." Modest was in a festive mood.

Olive took a big bite out of Captain Crunch's cap, then paused. "Wait. Just an hour ago, we were saving a ship from being hit by a torpedo. How did Poppy make these so quickly?"

Modest was busy munching on his second cookie. "We ordered these ahead of time," he said breezily.

"The torpedo was a test." Monica sounded pleased. "You all passed!"

All the Misfits stopped eating. James became solemn. "What do you mean?"

"NOCK needed confirmation that you were up for an assignment," Monica said casually. "So they set this up. The torpedo was real. However, had you failed to clear the ship, or if you hadn't been able to thwart the strike, it would have merely dented the side of the *O'Brien*."

"Captain Crunch was in on it." Modest reached for a third cookie. "He's one of us. The submarine explosion was his idea!"

Iggy flung her Captain Crunch cookie out the window. ("Thanks!" someone yelled from outside.)

"Excuse me," Iggy started angrily, "but am I the only one a little upset by all this?"

Personally, Olive didn't mind the test. She thought it

was kind of cool. Theo also looked okay with it, but James crossed his arms and scowled next to Iggy. However, it was Phil who was the most distressed.

"I was scared. I thought lives were in danger." Her voice was wobbly. "It was terrifying imagining what could happen if we failed . . . if *I* failed!"

"That's a great thing to feel," Monica said, not unkindly.

"Better to fail at a test than the real thing," Modest reassured them. "But you proved yourself, your teamwork, and your stellar skills."

James shook his head. "No, no, no. This wasn't a test. It was more like a pop quiz—only with battleships and a torpedo, and the threat of death. That's unprofessional!"

Iggy nodded in agreement. "James is right," she said in a rare show of unity.

"We *are* professionals," Monica LaMonica reminded them. "So are you. And there is no way NOCK would put you in the field without adequate operative training. This was the next level up from your SUCCESS Simulators: taking those skills and applying them in real time, in real life. You don't have a first-time doctor read a book, then operate on a patient, do you?"

No one answered.

"Would you want your pilot to go in the air before first training as a copilot?" Modest asked.

No one answered.

"We were monitoring you the entire time," Monica assured the Misfits. "Captain Crunch was there to make sure no one got hurt. The Red Hats? They were on a tour of San Francisco and told that they would be part of a live theater experience on the ship."

This did make sense, Olive had to admit. Even Iggy didn't look quite as mad as she had earlier.

Modest's eyes softened. "Not only did all of you pass, but you passed with flying colors, working together as a team. You truly succeeded at SUCCESS." He faced Monica. "Do you think they're ready for their first official assignment?"

Olive's breath caught. She crossed her fingers.

"I know they are," Monica answered.

Immediately, Olive's exhaustion evaporated. What would their first assignment be? *Will it be dangerous?* she wondered. She kind of hoped so. The idea of attempting a difficult and scary tightrope walk or trapeze trick always gave her the jitters, but in a good way.

Modest nodded. "Without further ado, then," he said, and a big screen lowered from the ceiling. The Misfits leaned in. No one was upset anymore. Finally, they would find out what they had been training for all this time. "Soon the gala fundraiser for the esteemed Dame Gloria Vanderwisp Foundation will be here at Foggy Manor. If it wasn't for Dame Gloria's generosity, the Reforming Arts School would cease to exist."

Everyone nodded. They knew this already, especially Olive, who lay awake at night worrying. It seemed RASCH's demise was the real threat after all.

From the display of swords, Monica removed a cutlass that once belonged to Blackbeard, the pirate. She pointed it at the screen, and an image of Dame Gloria appeared. She was as grand as ever, her hair fashioned in her signature tight white ringlets, with Winky, the cat brooch, worn as a barrette this time. Her smile looked sweet but practiced, and her violet eyes rivaled her huge jeweled necklace.

"*The Pirates of Penzance*," Monica began, "is the opera that will be performed at the gala. Some of the wealthiest people in San Francisco—and in the world—are scheduled to attend. However, as you Misfits have reported, a number of RASCH's biggest benefactors have begun to bow out. More will follow their example.

"Despite this, and the continued threat of the Bling King, Dame Gloria refuses to be intimidated. She will be announcing to the press that 'the show must go on!' That's because she has a personal investment in this."

A poster of *The Pirates of Penzance* flashed on the screen, showing a handsome man with a sharp chin and a thin mustache. "Let's be honest," Monica continued. "No one is coming to Foggy Island to see RASCH students perform." Iggy tried to disguise her sudden laugh as a hacking cough. "Instead, they are paying big money to bask in the presence of Dame Gloria *and* see soap-opera-star-turned-opera-singer Sterling Vanderwisp making his stage debut as the Pirate King. It is no coincidence that he happens to be Dame Gloria's only grandchild."

"Sterling's got a gambling problem and was fired from the last big soap opera he starred in," Modest chimed in. "If this opera can jump-start his career, it could mean a big break. Half the public wants him to succeed. The other half wants him to fail."

"How do we fit into all this?" James was on his third cookie.

Quickly, Modest rushed at Monica with an eighteenth-century double-edged spadroon. As the two began to sword-fight, Monica shouted over the clinking of metal, "Dame Gloria Vanderwisp is determined to make him a star at any cost. To maximize publicity, she will be wearing the famous Royal Rumpus necklace!"

"It's worth millions," Modest said, parrying an attack from Monica. "*Millions* and millions, in fact!"

The Misfits let out a collective gasp as the screen changed to feature a stunning necklace, breathtaking with its vibrant, clear colors and sparkling jewels the size of Ping-Pong balls. "The Royal Rumpus consists of several flawless gems, including a brownish-yellow diamond weighing over 442.07 carats known as the Aphrodite Diamond—the rarest gem in the world. This necklace is seldom seen in public," Monica informed them. "Dame Gloria seeks to shame those patrons who refuse to attend the gala by implying that they are cowards when she shows up wearing the Royal Rumpus."

"However, NOCK has been tipped off that the Royal Rumpus will be targeted by thieves." Modest made a low lunge at Monica, who skillfully jumped over his sword.

"The Bling King," Phil whispered solemnly.

"The Bling King Ring," James agreed. "He must have a ring of minions working for him. One can't become king all on their own."

"So, you want us to capture the Bling King?" Iggy asked hopefully.

This was bigger than Olive had imagined. Her mind was spinning. Imagine capturing a world-famous jewel thief!

"Dame Gloria will have her bodyguards, and extra security will be watching the Royal Rumpus at all times." Monica pretended to stab Modest in the heart. After he faux-fell to the floor, she rested her foot on his chest and continued, "Misfits, your job is to go undercover as backup and report any suspicious activity. You've already got the perfect cover since you're RASCH students."

Iggy couldn't be more obvious in her disappointment. "We're just backup?"

Modest leaped to his feet and brushed off his jump-suit. "No assignment is too big or too small for NOCK. All jobs are important when it means helping to prevent chaos, assisting in catching lawbreakers, and protecting the citizenry."

Modest and Monica seemed pleased as Iggy nodded glumly. James and Phil looked thoughtful, while Theo appeared torn. As for Olive, she tried to smile at Modest and Monica, but inside she was secretly disappointed that the Misfits weren't going to do more.

Anything to save RASCH, Olive reminded herself. If the Misfits could help as backup, then she was going to be the absolute best backup she could be. Olive recalled Mimi telling her, "Backup singers are unsung heroes. Without them, most songs would sound flat."

25.
A PURPOSE

With only three weeks before the *Pirates of Penzance* performance, Sunny summoned all the RASCHers into an assembly in front of the manor. Looking around the great expanse of lawn at the other students, Olive wondered who was NOCK and who was not. It was impossible to tell.

Yash used a foghorn to divert everyone's attention to Sunny, who was standing on the mansion's stairs. "With this year's gala, our mission is to showcase our talents!" the dean began. Olive breathed in the fragrant blooms of the nearby Chantilly snapdragon flowers that Brood was trimming. "Our collective performances will encourage the gala guests to donate generously to the Dame Gloria Vanderwisp Foundation, which, in turn, helps fund RASCH.

"Each one of you will have a special role to play at this year's gala, and I thank you for your support in advance!" Sunny nodded toward Yash, who began to clap as if it was an afterthought. "Now, please listen as I give you your assignments. . . ."

All the pods were involved in one way or another, including those who were performing onstage, backstage, and in the orchestra pit. Others were in charge of wardrobe, posters, programs, and so on. As for the Misfits, they had a gala assignment, too.

"Pod 101 will help as backup ushers," Sunny said, looking pleased.

"Backup ushers?" Primrose whispered snidely from behind the Misfits. "Like that's even a thing. Try not to botch that." Her pod was in charge of flower arrangements.

Iggy glared in her direction, but Olive couldn't help but agree with Primrose, however rude she was.

"Backup ushers?!" Theo complained that evening over dinner. He bit into a buttermilk biscuit flecked with caramelized ginger. Given RASCH's precarious financial situation, Butter Bakery breads and pastries were now rationed to one per student for each meal. "Where's the fun, the danger, the glory in that?"

"That's just our cover," James reminded him. "We'll be NOCK's eyes and ears."

"Maybe this is another test?" Phil ventured. She was still slightly shaken from the last one.

"Well, whatever it is, we're helping to catch a world-class criminal," Olive said, trying to sound pleased. She didn't want to tell the others that she was disappointed, too. It would be nice to at least say that they had a part in capturing the Bling King.

"It's kinda scary," James reluctantly admitted. "We could be inches away from one of the most wanted criminals in the world. I don't know that I'm ready for danger like that."

Olive gave him a sympathetic smile. She remembered how he'd frozen when Smote and his crew had attacked them. Even though James had kept his cool during Code Bagel and had been pivotal to their success, the idea of putting oneself in danger was difficult for him.

"If we do our jobs and spot anything fishy, we notify the authorities. We're not expected to capture any criminals, and especially not one as big as the Bling King," Olive reassured him.

"NOCK wouldn't have put us on the case at all if they didn't think we were up to it," Phil reasoned. "Besides, we've got each other's backs."

James looked at Iggy, who winked and said begrudgingly, "Yeah, I'd save your life, but only if it means extra credit."

When James broke out in a smile, the other Misfits did, too. They hadn't come this far to fail.

Later, the group huddled in the safety of the Laundry Room. Poppy was testing a new recipe, and earlier Auntie Winnie had given Theo a spiced caramel cake to share with the others.

"What do we know of the Bling King so far?" Theo asked. There were six slices of cake and five Misfits.

"He's been at large for a while," James said, unaware of the frosting on his nose. "The Bling King always goes after high-profile gems. He's known to target celebrities and chic jewelry stores and, most recently, museum pieces."

"So his previous robberies were just a warm-up for the Royal Rumpus," Olive theorized. She noted Iggy was eyeing the one remaining piece of cake. Poppy had outdone herself again.

Phil agreed. "He's not just after the jewelry—he's after *glory*. That's why the Bling King leaves a calling card. He's showing off. It's an ego thing, and the Royal Rumpus is the most expensive piece of jewelry in the world. Dame Gloria hasn't even worn it publicly in decades—"

"And when she does, she expects attention, too!" Iggy quickly added as she observed Olive.

"The Bling King and Dame Gloria are a match made in heaven." Olive stared boldly back at Iggy.

The two grinned at each other, then at the same time both lunged at the last piece of cake.

Except it had vanished!

"How are you going to find the Bling King if you can't even find this," James asked, triumphantly holding up the last slice.

Theo was now unrolling a map of the Foggy Manor theater as he leaned back in his antique barber's chair. "With Dame Gloria's and the Bling King's oversized egos, there's sure to be a showdown," he said, laughing.

156

Earlier, Modest had presented special chairs to each Misfit for good luck. It was easy to tell whose was whose. With the cake gone, James was sitting in his polished wood banker's chair practicing deep breathing to help with his anxiety. "What if the Bling King shows up and there's real danger after all?" James sounded anxious.

"Then it's up to us to protect Dame Gloria and the Royal Rumpus!" Iggy said, kicking back in her black leather recliner. She punched her fist up into the air.

"Not really," Phil reminded her. She rolled her high-tech ergonomic chair into her workshop and called out, "We're just extra eyes and ears, remember?"

At that, a quiet sense of relief came over Olive as she sank deeper into her purple beanbag chair. As much as she wanted to prove herself, she wasn't sure if she was ready to fight the Bling King or his ring of supporters.

Still, as NOCK agents masquerading as backup ushers, the Misfits took their training seriously. They needed to blend in, move quickly, and master their ComChom communications. Plus they were expected to be both stealthy and acutely aware of everything going on at once while ushering people to their seats if needed.

With the gala coming up quickly, the Misfits dove into last-minute training. They started doing three simulations a day in the Laundry Room. Meanwhile, in the gymkhana, Modest led them through obstacle course after obstacle course, while Monica critiqued the fluidity of their movements. Through RASCH's teacher exchange program, the Misfits worked with a drama coach who was unaware that they were secret NOCK agents. While they learned the fundamentals of acting and putting on a convincing cover, Modest taught her drama students square-dancing.

Olive enjoyed acting—pretending she was someone she was not. There was a certain familiarity to it. Until recently, she'd felt like she was only pretending to be a NOCK agent and that they'd selected her by accident, instead of Primrose or Zeke, maybe. Then again, perhaps she had been an elite secret operative all along, and the old invisible, klutzy Olive was actually the impostor?

Her thoughts kept going back and forth like a ball at a tennis match.

What if she failed her first real mission? Would she return to being ordinary Olive? She couldn't even begin to imagine that.

With the gala a week away, the team was discussing ways to cover a large venue, when Phil piped up from her workshop. "Misfits, I'm ready!"

Modest and Monica emerged from their faculty lounge, both carrying oversized coffee cups, and watched with pride as the team gathered around Phil, who was handing out her newest invention: FoggyGogs. "These allow you to see through fog and smoke. They're an updated version of the prescription goggles Yash always wears while driving BoBu."

"I thought you were making weapons!" Iggy didn't hide her disappointment.

"I prefer to think of what I've invented as accessories because they will enhance our skills." Phil helped James adjust his FoggyGogs over his glasses. "I suppose some could be categorized as weapons, though they are made for defense."

She held up what looked like a tube of ChapStick. "Everything was inspired by stuff you normally carry around, so nothing looks suspicious. This is Stink Spray. If someone is getting too close to you, you can spray it on yourself to repel them."

Phil sprayed some into the air. Olive and Iggy pinched their noses.

"It smells like the worst fart ever," James said, gagging.

"Thank you!" Phil looked pleased. "Also, if you want to use it to track a target, one spray and they'll stink until they take a shower. Three sprays and no one will want to get near them." She passed around a basket of nose clamps. "In case you don't want to smell the stink."

To the Misfits' delight, Phil had also created other dazzling accessories, including a bracelet that held a sleep-inducing mist that activated upon contact (Snooze Vapors), the Ultra Stick to jam doors shut or lock shoes to the ground, and a modified Slinky that, when stretched, created a trip wire, coiled spring, or rope.

After they were done oohing and aahing, and testing their accessories, Modest passed around ordinary-looking fanny packs.

"For your accessories," Monica explained.

Modest strapped one around his hips and posed, showing it off. "They look small, but that's just an optical illusion. One time I put several jars of dill pickles in mine," he boasted.

Olive strapped her own around her waist and stowed all her accessories inside, watching as the other Misfits did the same.

"Oh!" Phil remembered. "One more thing." She assigned smartphones to everyone. They were much lighter than they looked, and Olive was amazed by how pliable hers was.

"These are Misfit versions of phones," Phil continued as Theo folded his into a paper airplane and Iggy rolled hers into a tube. "They do everything a cell phone does, plus so much more. I'll be creating exclusive apps that are accessible only on your devices."

But as her teammates tested their new accessories, Olive still wondered: With all their training, plus tools for SUC-CESS, would that be enough to help save RASCH? She touched her fanny pack protectively and crossed all her fingers.

26.
SWASHBUCKLER

The night before the big day, none of the Misfits could sleep. Not even Theo, who was usually snoring by 8:30 p.m.

There was nothing more they could do. The Misfits had done a group inventory of their accessories, practiced fighting and falling, and reviewed the protocol: safety first, defend and disarm, constant communication. They had doubled up on the simulator sessions, physical training, and team building. As undercover backup ushers backing up the professional security teams, they pledged to help ensure the safety of Dame Gloria and the Royal Rumpus, and, in doing so, help secure the future of RASCH.

Before turning off her lights, Olive fetched the orange suitcase from the wardrobe. She retrieved her mother's fluffy pink bathrobe and slipped it on. The hem touched the floor, and the sleeves draped past her fingers. It was so soft, and it smelled just like Dr. Cobin Zang. Olive wrapped the robe around her tight, imagining this was a hug from her mom.

If her parents knew what their daughter was up to, would they be proud?

She stuck her hands deep in the robe's pockets and was surprised to feel a piece of paper. Olive unfolded it and let out a gasp when she found a letter addressed to her.

My Darling Daughter,

I am so proud of you and all the skills you are learning at school. I'm sorry I'm not around as much as we'd both like, but I love you more than anything. I'll see you soon.

—Mom

P.S. If you believe in something, keep trying, and don't be afraid to fail.

Olive reread it twice. Her heart thudded in her chest. How did her mother know that she would take the wrong suitcase?

There was something off about the letter, though. Olive looked at it again, studying the swoops that formed each word. . . .

Then she realized: This wasn't her mother's careful handwriting. It was Mimi's. Her grandmother must have written this for Olive's mother when she was a kid.

Could you feel happy and sad at the same time? Olive missed her grandmother so much that it hurt. Yet, with the note, it was almost like Mimi was there with her, encouraging her granddaughter on her very first mission. As she read her grandmother's words again, Olive's anxiety fell away and was replaced with a growing confidence.

She tucked it under her pillow, and with the bathrobe wrapped around her, her eyelids began to get heavy. There would be plenty to worry about tomorrow, but for tonight, sleep was what Olive needed most.

By the next afternoon, the entire island had been transformed into an elaborate pirates' paradise. Sunny had named the daylily the official flower of the gala, and blood-red blooms with yellow centers appeared everywhere. Brood had hung skull and crossbones flags all around Foggy Island. And, of course, every RASCH student was dressed as a pirate. The costume pod had outdone themselves. Olive loved her silky white shirt, red vest with brass buttons, and simple black headband. Even Brood was in full pirate attire, and several people complimented him on his stubble and surly look.

The Misfits reported to the dock as soon as the first guests began to arrive, where their incredibly gleeful dean was pacing. Sunny kept breaking into fits of giggles as fleets of yachts, motorboats, and sailboats flying skull and crossbones flags motored toward the island.

"Ma'am," Yash quickly reminded her. The toy parrot perched on her shoulder kept flopping over. "They're just people."

"They aren't just people—they're celebrities!" Sunny insisted, looking starstruck.

Olive supposed this was somewhat true. Despite an ornery group of benefactors who had elected not to come, Dame Gloria Vanderwisp's presence—and the lure of seeing the Royal Rumpus in person—had managed to sell out the gala, making this *the* event of the season. It promised a once-in-a-lifetime sighting of the most expensive necklace in the world, and most were willing to brave the possibility of the Bling King being among them. Though truth be told, some were hoping he would make an appearance. How exciting that would be!

The press was in full force. To boost publicity for RASCH and the gala, Dame Gloria had requested the presence of news outlets, entertainment shows, reality TV crews, and even a personal video documentarian. Photographers, videographers, and newscasters were all grouped at the end of the dock, jostling for the best camera angles as the boats sailed toward Foggy Island.

While they watched the remaining guests arrive, Olive stopped Theo from accidentally putting Stink Spray on his chapped lips. Iggy kept insisting that a real sword would go better with her outfit. James was fidgeting so much that Olive worried that he'd fall into the water. And Phil was quiet, deep in thought.

When the guests were ready to be ushered inside, the Misfits were called to the mansion. A plush red carpet led from the dock, down the cobblestone path, and up the massive marble stairs of Foggy Manor. A huge black velvet banner hung over the entrance, with glittery gold letters announcing, DAME GLORIA VANDERWISP FOUNDATION PIRATES' GALA TO BENEFIT RASCH.

Security was as tight as a new tube of toothpaste. Every person stepping foot on the island was photographed twice, once by the paparazzi and once by the police. Foggy Island was soon swarming with private guards in uniform, police in uniform and undercover as civilians, RASCHers and catering staff dressed as pirates, and VIP guests dressed in fancy swashbuckling attire and tuxedos and ball gowns.

Going mostly unnoticed were five nervous undercover NOCK agents. Olive checked her fanny pack for what seemed like the hundredth time, just to make sure everything was still there.

In the mansion's foyer was a magnificent array of stunning appetizers and desserts. The most striking of all were the Tiny Treasures Treasure Chests from Butter Bakery. Olive had glimpsed Poppy and Auntie Winnie painstakingly making the mini chocolate treasure chests filled with brownie bottom cheesecakes and topped with sugar gems, gummy skulls, and edible pearls, and she was as proud of their desserts as if she had made them herself.

As the Misfits glided between the gala attendees, keeping an eye out for anything suspicious, the RASCH fanfare trumpeters signaled the arrival of the guest of honor. Everyone whirled around to face the entrance. Olive was in the rear of the room but wove through the crowd, even pirouetting when necessary, to get up to the front.

When Dame Gloria finally waltzed into the foyer, she could barely be seen under the layers of emerald-green fabric that swirled around her. A bejeweled crown was secured atop her hair, and Olive spotted Winky on her left sleeve, his emerald-green eyes twinkling. However, the rest of Dame Gloria's outfit paled in comparison to her necklace.

Iggy gasped into her ComChom, "Do you see what I see?!"

The Royal Rumpus, with its colorful jewels anchored by the famous Aphrodite Diamond at its center, sparkled and glowed on Dame Gloria's neck amid the camera flashes. Both she and the Royal Rumpus were more mesmerizing in person than in any photos or film. The guest of honor was flanked by an army of security guards wearing slick black suits, mirrored sunglasses, and snooty attitudes. When Sunny strayed too close, one guard growled at her, causing the RASCH dean to scream and Yash to growl back.

166

Dame Gloria raised a dainty hand with a ring on every finger. Instantly, the room went silent. When she spoke, her voice rang with an authority that surprised Olive.

"Thank you, all of you, for joining me this evening for the Dame Gloria Vanderwisp Foundation Pirates' Gala!" She was showered with a flurry of applause, which the grande dame waved away gracefully. "I hope you will follow me into the theater for *The Pirates of Penzance* in just a moment. I've heard it's a real production to . . . *sea!*" She winked heartily, and the room lit up with appreciative laughter.

That was the ushers' cue. With the other Misfits, Olive began directing guests to the theater and then assisted the primary ushers in escorting everyone to their seats.

After everyone was seated, the Misfits gathered at the far wall of the theater, where they had a good view of the audience. In time with the music, Sunny danced onto the stage. Her bright yellow gown and a feathered pirate's hat contrasted nicely against the red velvet curtains. Looking radiant, she leaned into the microphone. "Welcome to RASCH's production of *The Pirates of Penzance,* with our very special guest star . . . Sterling Vanderwisp! On behalf of world-renowned icon Dame Gloria Vanderwisp"—Sunny motioned to the opera box, where the spotlight now illuminated Dame Gloria blowing kisses to the auditorium—"thank you for your generous donations!" Sunny finished, and the whole theater applauded.

The lights dimmed, the audience hushed, and the orchestra pod began playing music that Olive had been hearing for weeks while they rehearsed all over the island. During the show, the ushers were invited to stay and enjoy the opera. However, the Misfits had other places to be.

On the lookout for suspicious characters, Olive crept toward Dame Gloria's opera box as her grandson waved a sword and sang onstage. Even though his voice was lacking, he was surprisingly agile.

Nearby, a cluster of undercover cops . . . looked like a cluster of undercover cops. When one glanced her way, Olive stuck her finger in her nose, and he turned away.

Closer to the opera box, one of the four bodyguards frowned when Olive got a little too close. "Dame Gloria is not giving autographs. Scram, kid."

"Sorry," Olive said, meek as a mouse, her head bowed. The drama lessons were paying off. She smiled slightly as she backed away into the shadows. At her old school, Olive hated not being noticed. Here, it was an asset.

Just then, James's voice came through on the EarBuzz. "Alert! Alert! Suspicious pirates sneaking around the lobby!"

"Modest? Monica?" Olive knew they weren't supposed to leave their posts. She paused near the opera box. "Advise immediately!"

There was only silence from the faculty. Olive's stomach dropped. Silence from Modest and Monica meant it was time for Plan B.

27.
I AM NOT AFRAID

In record speed, the Misfits converged in the lobby that connected the theater and the massive Foggy Manor foyer. Sure enough, they spotted three pirates acting suspiciously. One bearded pirate had *Triste in Thought,* a foot-tall bronze sculpture of Remy Triste posing like Rodin's *The Thinker,* under his arms. Across the way, a large pirate was tucking something into his bulging coat. A petite pirate was trying to force a hand-carved mantel clock into her duffel bag. When they spotted the Misfits, the crooks jumped.

"Shiver me timbers and scatter!" the bearded one yelled to the others. "Wee kiddies are afoot!"

"Get them!" Iggy cried, racing toward the biggest one.

This was their moment. It was as if all their training was coming into play—the leaps, the twirls, the falling, the running, the throwing. In a heartbeat, they were chasing the thieves, who were now heading out of the mansion and into the fog, toward the DONUT TRESPASS! area. The sun was setting, and visibility was low as the fog began to roll in.

"FoggyGogs on!" Phil broadcast via the ComChoms. "Misfits, this is not a test! This is the real thing!"

"Modest! Monica!" Olive called. "There are three thieving pirates making their way toward the 'Donut Trespass' sign. We are in pursuit. Please advise!"

Someone had cut the chain-link fence, making it easy to get through. Though the pirates were fast, the Misfits were faster, thanks to all their training. It didn't take long to catch up to the thieves.

"I am not afraid. I am not afraid. I am not afraid," James chanted as he closed in on the bearded pirate, who was cradling the statue of Remy Triste like a baby.

Olive almost got hit when the pirate tossed the Remy Triste statue aside. He pivoted and, with both hands raised in the air, roared at James like a bear.

"In pursuit of the crook who's in pursuit of James," Olive reported into her ComChom.

"I am not afraid!" James screamed unconvincingly at the bearded man.

In a seamless move, Olive reached for her Snooze Vapors, aimed, and fired. Time seemed to move at a turtle's pace as the mist released from her bracelet, and then . . .

Thud!

As if in slow motion, James fell gently to the ground.

"James!" Olive yelled.

"I am not afraid," he murmured before falling asleep.

Olive couldn't move. Now everything was happening so fast it was hard to think straight. She lurched back like *she* had been hit, but it was in fact Olive who had hit James with the Snooze Vapors.

Iggy ran past them, chasing after the large pirate. "Stop!" she cried. "Or else!"

The pirate stopped and wriggled a bushy eyebrow. "Or else what, ye scurvy dog?"

"Or else this!" Iggy held up her fists.

"Whoa, whoa, whoa!" he said, dropping his pirate accent. "Careful, girlie, or you'll hurt someone!"

Using Modest Cusak's patented sideswipe twirl, followed by Monica's infamous double uppercut, swing-around, and ankle-trip, Iggy had the thief on the ground in no time. She quickly tied him up with the Time-Out String.

Just then, Theo raced by, chasing the petite pirate carrying the duffel bag. "Stop, this is the police!" he cried, using the voice changer on his ComChom.

The woman froze. When she did, Phil whispered from behind a nearby tree, "*Psst,* I'll hide you from the cops!"

"Thanks!" the pirate said brightly, tiptoeing toward Phil . . . and stepping right into the Ultra Stick. Theo and Phil high-fived as the pirate struggled to move.

By now, Olive's adrenaline was on overdrive, and she propelled herself toward James. He was on the ground, snoring peacefully as the bearded pirate thief stood over him, looking confused. Pushing off with her left leg, Olive executed a grand jeté and struck the pirate's shoulder. And as the thief began to topple, she emptied her Time-Out String, wrapping him up nicely like a present for the authorities.

Iggy, Phil, and Theo looked as shocked as Olive felt.

They had done it. They had actually done it! They had three thieves, captured and ready for questioning by the authorities. And just in time. All of a sudden, police and security guards rushed toward the Misfits. It seemed Modest and Monica had finally let them know what was going on.

"Freeze!" ordered the police.

With her hands in the air, Iggy shouted, "We're the good guys!" Olive, Theo, and Phil slowly put their hands up, too.

Beside them, James sat up and rubbed his eyes. "Did I miss anything?"

Guilt welled up in Olive, yet she was surprised to hear herself say, "You just fell asleep. It was the weirdest thing." Before she could continue, the press and authorities descended on the area.

28.
DAME GLORIA

As the police hauled the thieving pirates into custody, they also rounded up five innocent-looking students.

"Remember to deflect their questions," Olive whispered to the others over the ComChoms. "They can't know we're NOCK and what our real mission is—as eyes and ears on the lookout for the Bling King. That we have captured these thieves is a bonus, but our cover can't be blown!"

The Misfits readied their excuses for the police, drawing on their drama lessons. . . .

"I'm just a backup usher."

"I was lost."

"Can I call my mom?"

"Can I call my father's lawyers?"

When James employed fake tears in full force, he had the

police apologizing to him and offering him a lollipop, which he happily accepted.

Olive kept smiling brightly at James, trying to mask the guilt that was weighing heavily on her shoulders. In her mind, she couldn't stop replaying the sight of him toppling over midfight, all because of *her* mistake.

"What?" he asked suspiciously, his voice still a little groggy. "Why are you looking at me like that?"

"I'm just happy you're here!"

"You're weird." James yawned, then bit into his lollipop. "Why am I so sleepy?"

Simultaneously, the pirate thieves were being grilled by the authorities. They came up with whoppers that no one believed, describing how children leaped through the air and dropped out of trees, and used slingshots and a spray that immobilized them.

"We're actors!" the petite pirate shouted as she was being handcuffed.

"You're arresting me for filling my pockets with desserts?" the big pirate protested.

He was stealing Poppy's pastries? Olive was confused.

"We were hired to cause mischief!" the bearded one insisted. He pointed in the distance, to something behind them all. "Besides, shouldn't you be over there?!"

At once, they all turned toward Foggy Manor, where dark smoke was billowing from the mansion's windows.

Instantly, the police hollered as they scrambled to organize, but it was the Misfits who didn't hesitate, immediately bolting toward the gala. They burst into the foyer and ran through the theater lobby to find clouds of smoke pouring out the doors.

Guests were starting to trickle from the theater, coughing. Olive spotted Yash dragging Sunny by one arm.

The Misfits slipped on their FoggyGogs, grabbed cloth napkins from the food tables to cover their mouths, and, dodging the guests, ran toward the source of the smoke to get a lock on what was happening.

Through her FoggyGogs, Olive could make out more pirates and finely dressed guests in a panic as they jostled left and right, pushing toward the exits. Olive fought against the crowd toward where she last saw Dame Gloria. By the time she got to the opera box, Theo was already waiting, shaking his head.

"She's gone," he said.

"Misfits, it's me." They could hear Monica over their Ear-Buzzes. "Modest and I fell off the grid during the commotion, but we're locking in on Dame Gloria's whereabouts."

"We're back at the theater, awaiting instruction," Olive reported.

"We need all Misfits on deck," Monica ordered. "Help get the guests outside in a calm

and orderly fashion, then report to Sunny's office ASAP."

So there they were, lowly backup ushers. It took almost an hour to shepherd everyone to the lawn, away from the smoke and chaos. Half the guests were surprisingly calm given everything that had happened, while the other half were in tears. Olive never expected to see so many sobbing pirates.

A scream cut through the crying, followed by a panicked woman shouting, "My diamond necklace! It's gone!"

"Was it the Bling King?" someone asked, excitedly. "Is he here?"

"The Bling King? Where? I want to get a picture!" another person said, sounding giddy as the woman whose necklace was stolen was whisked away by security.

By the time the Misfits arrived at Sunny's office, most of the smoke had cleared out of the building. The room was packed—and in the middle of it all was a tiny figure swathed in green.

"I want my necklace back *now*!" Dame Gloria Vander-wisp bellowed. "I was assured that the Royal Rumpus would be safe! And what's even worse is that Winky is missing!"

"Who's Winky?" Olive overheard a police officer ask.

"Granny G, they're doing what they can." A surprisingly composed Sterling Vanderwisp tried to calm her. He was still gripping his stage sword. When he laid a hand on Dame Gloria's shoulder, she flicked it away. "Anyway, the necklace is insured," he noted. "You'll get money for it, right?"

"Oh, you airheaded boy," she snapped. "It's not about the money! The Royal Rumpus and Winky are what I love the most in the whole wide world!" Sterling flinched. "This clown has *ruined* everything!" His grandmother flung something at him. Olive peered out from the corner of the office to get a better look.

It was a Bling King calling card. Her heart sank as she took it in, the printed golden crown winking up at them all. She glanced at Iggy and Theo, who looked just as upset.

Dame Gloria pointed accusingly at Sunny. "This is your fault!"

"It's not her fault," Yash growled as she adjusted her parrot.

"I am so sorry," Sunny said tearfully. "Dame Gloria, we will do everything we can to work with law enforcement and make sure the Royal Rumpus and Winky are found."

Dame Gloria fixed her violet eyes on the dean with a glower so powerful that several police officers shuddered. "Sunny O'Moa, if I hadn't had my gala here, this would *not* have happened. If Winky and the Royal Rumpus are not returned by the end of the month, I will see to it that your beloved RASCH is shut down. Permanently!"

29.
RUBY

Defeated, the Misfits changed out of their pirate costumes before trudging to the Laundry Room to face Modest and Monica. The walk to their wing was painfully quiet. Their first mission, and they'd failed spectacularly.

When they filed past the portrait of Dame Gloria and entered, they were shocked to find a third person waiting for them. Modest, Monica, and the stranger were huddled in the middle of the Laundry Room.

"What's she doing here?" Iggy pointed at the woman. "I thought this room was off-limits."

"Ruby Lopez is one of us," Monica said matter-of-factly.

Modest gave Ruby a double thumbs-up.

The woman kept her hands on her belt. "San Francisco police chief and NOCK," she said by way of introduction.

Monica explained, "There are lots of NOCK operatives. Most are in the background. Some are embedded in various

179

government agencies, like Ruby here. Only a handful of our most elite are in the field actively interacting with suspects."

"Kids, sit down and take a breath. You're not in trouble . . . ," Ruby began, her raspy voice serious, and then she slapped the table, adding, "Yet." She laughed. "I'm here to bring you up to speed on what happened, and to ask questions." She circled the room, studying each Misfit one by one as they tried not to squirm. Only Iggy looked her straight in the eye.

Olive noted that Ruby matched Modest's height, though her auburn pixie cut made her look slightly less intimidating.

"Before we begin, you need to know who I am." Ruby turned to Monica. "You wanna tell them?"

"The chief and I first met in the ring many years ago. It was a championship bout." Monica looked wistful at the memory. "Ruby is an excellent boxer."

"Not as good as Monica LaMonica," Ruby said generously. "She knocked me down in round five."

"But first Ruby gave me a dislocated shoulder." The two old friends looked at each other with mutual admiration.

Ruby loosened her collar and parked herself in Theo's barber chair. "Nice place you got here," she said, putting her feet up. "At the precinct, it's all wobbly metal chairs. When I first got whiff of the Royal Rumpus being trotted out from the mothballs, I knew it would be a target.

"I heard the mark was making an appearance at Foggy Manor, and I instantly thought of my friend Ms. LaMonica here. I needed to put a team in place on the island. Imagine my surprise when she told me she already had one . . . and it was kids!"

The Misfits sat just a little taller, though Olive could not shake the shame that had weighed upon her since she failed to stop the Bling King. Ruby went on, "The problem was that the jewel thieves had two teams of their own, which we didn't know until now. There were the real pros, the Bling King Ring, plus decoys—local actors who were told that my officers were also performance artists, and that they were all

in on a large skit." Ruby got up from the chair. Her voice softened. "Kids, don't be too hard on yourselves. This was a big job. Bigger than any of us expected."

Like the others, Olive sat stunned as Ruby laid it out for them. "The real pros not only left with the Royal Rumpus, but also helped themselves to other valuable jewels, like they were showing off."

"For publicity," James said slowly. "They knew the gala would be covered by the press. They wanted the world to know what they did."

"Copy that!" Ruby touched her nose and pointed to James, who looked pleased with himself. "The good news is that the gems are so hot it's impossible for them to leave the city. As it is, we still can't figure out how the jewels got off the island."

Phil looked upset. "Are we in trouble? Do the police think we had something to do with the heist?"

Ruby shook her head. "There was some talk about students being involved, but I managed to spin it that you were just in the wrong place at the wrong time with the wrong people. Besides, no one can believe that youngsters captured fake thieves. That's what makes you our special weapon."

"This isn't even fair," Iggy complained. "Dame Gloria was warned that she *shouldn't* wear the jewels to the gala. And now RASCH is in trouble because she didn't listen!"

"Now, now," Modest said, trying to calm Iggy. "The school needed a gigantic fundraiser before all this even started. Even though she can be persnickety, Dame Gloria has RASCH's best interests at heart." His normally cheerful demeanor became serious. "It *was* up to both NOCK and the police to keep the jewels safe, after all."

Olive could see what he meant. But silently, she couldn't help agreeing with Iggy.

Monica checked the clock. "Turn on the television."

At the top of the hour, the news headlined with a banner that read, *Royal Rumpus—Biggest Jewel Heist of the Century.* The news anchor, whose blond hair was fashioned with a swoop in the front, winked at the camera as a photo of Dame Gloria wearing her necklace loomed large on the screen behind him.

"Well, shiver me timbers! The quarter-billion-dollar Royal Rumpus necklace, three other multimillion-dollar necklaces, and Dame Gloria Vanderwisp's black diamond cat brooch were plundered during the Pirates of Penzance *opera at Foggy Manor on Foggy Island in the San Francisco Bay.*

"At an exclusive fundraiser for the Dame Gloria Vanderwisp Foundation, the reclusive socialite emerged wearing her famed necklace, only to have it stolen by, we can only assume, the Bling King. And this is despite a virtual army guarding it!" The anchor winked at the camera again. *"More updates to come in the next hour! In the meantime, everyone's gone cat crazy for KittyKon! Take a meow at some of these cosplay, er . . . catplay costumes. . . ."*

Monica shut off the TV. "The Royal Rumpus must be recovered within three weeks."

She didn't have to say anything else. Everyone knew what was on the line. If the priceless necklace wasn't found, RASCH would cease to exist.

30.
BLAME GAME

The tension in the Laundry Room was coiled as tightly as a rattlesnake ready to strike. Even though Police Chief Ruby Lopez had assured the Misfits that it wasn't their fault the Royal Rumpus was stolen, Olive and the others still felt responsible. If they hadn't pursued the fake thieves and steered security away from the show, the Bling King might not have made his move.

Despite his playful tartan plaid jumpsuit, Modest looked serious. "We need to break down what happened and why."

"I'll tell you what happened." Iggy motioned to the other Misfits. "They messed up."

Olive sat up with a start. She knew Iggy sometimes said things she didn't mean when she was angry, but—

"Hey, it was *you* who said 'Get them,'" James shot back at Iggy.

"And it was *you* who said there were suspicious pirates in the lobby!" Iggy shouted angrily.

"How was I supposed to know they were decoys?" James had both fists clenched.

"Oh, right. You were too busy sleeping!" Iggy said bitterly.

Olive's shocked silence started to feel like it was choking her.

In a soft voice, Phil said, "This is all my fault. If the ComChoms hadn't malfunctioned and cut us off from the Laundry Room, Modest and Monica could have advised us."

Everyone stared at Phil, who was on the verge of tears.

"I hit James with the Snooze Vapors!" Olive confessed, hoping to deflect the attention from her best friend.

"What?!" James looked at Olive, his eyes wide. "How could you do that to me?"

She started to explain, but Monica poked Modest. "Tell them."

His broad shoulders slumped. "It's possible that I accidentally turned off the transmitter and cut off your communications to and from the Laundry Room, and us. It was an innocent error, of course."

Olive saw Phil's body tense. "Operator error cut off our communication? I thought it was my fault the mission failed! The pressure was so . . . so . . ."

Phil ran out of the room. Olive stood to go after her but was stopped by James's harsh glare.

"It was an accident." Olive's words tumbled over each other. "I should have told you sooner."

"That's for sure!" James headed toward the door.

"It was an accident!" Olive said again, now remembering what Mimi had always said when she messed up. *Take responsibility.* "James, I'm sorry. . . ." But by then he was gone.

Monica and Modest were still as statues. Iggy and Theo gave each other sideways glances but remained silent. "I may as well leave, too," Olive said glumly. She hoped that someone would try to stop her, but no one did.

After the gala, Sunny took to sobbing through the mansion corridors and around the island as Yash trailed her with a box of tissues and a tiny trash can. Olive did her best to avoid them, lest she start crying, too. In the span of twenty-four hours, she had gone from being on top of the world as a promising NOCK operative to turning back into a nobody.

What was worse, Olive had taken down one of her own—and confessed only when the guilt became too much to bear. That's not what a NOCK operative does. That's not what a Misfit does. That's not what a *friend* does. Olive wouldn't blame them if they lost respect for her. After all, she had lost respect for herself.

As long as RASCH was afloat, the Misfits were still required to show up to class. Only Iggy had the guts to ask if they would be helping with the case to recover the Royal Rumpus, though she looked like she already knew the answer.

"Ah, no," Modest had replied sadly. "Law enforcement is taking the lead. We must assume NOCK will let us know when we can be of assistance. Besides"—he cast a knowing glance at the dejected faces in the room—"the Misfits have other things to work on at the moment."

With morale at an all-time low, Monica and Modest did all they could to rally the team. NOCK training continued, but any enthusiasm and energy the Misfits once had were gone, just like the Royal Rumpus. At mealtimes, Theo joined Zeke and his buddies, and the others sat by themselves.

Olive had almost forgotten what it was like to be alone. Her heart ached more than ever.

At night, she continued climbing out her window in the mansion. Sometimes she'd scurry all the way up to the roof's ridge, sitting on one of the bigger gargoyles. Mimi always said it was a wonderful thing that her only grandchild wasn't afraid of heights.

What Olive was afraid of, though, was that she had lost the only true friends she had ever known. To make things worse, if the school was shuttered, then not only would she have to leave, but so would every RASCH student—and for some this was their only home.

In her short time at Foggy Manor, it had started to feel like Olive's home, too.

A full week after the gala, authorities were still no closer to recovering the Royal Rumpus, Winky, or the other jewels. When Olive left the dorm early one evening, James had his nose buried in a book, Phil looked bored as she tapped on her rings, and Iggy had her door shut with a *Leave Me Alone* note taped to it.

No one asked where Olive was going. Did they even care? It was as if the months of training, bonding, and having the best times of their lives had never happened.

The fog hadn't rolled in yet, and a dinner cruise boat was sailing around the bay. Some of the passengers waved toward Foggy Island, and Olive observed several RASCHers hooting and hollering back. She stared at them wistfully. Sometimes she forgot NOCK was special and that most students were blissfully unaware that school was in danger of closing.

Olive could feel her ComChom against her teeth. She liked how it connected her to the other Misfits, even if they didn't talk to each other anymore.

Up the pathway, Theo and Zeke exited Butter Bakery carrying bags of pastries, probably for the Community Outreach Center. Zeke greeted her warmly as they walked by, but when Theo would not meet her glance, Olive stopped in her tracks as sadness weighed on her like an anchor. Now, instead of hanging out with the Misfits, Olive filled her time talking to the swans, working on acrobatics, and visiting the bakery. With Theo and Zeke gone, she made her way up to Butter Bakery and opened the door.

The air was laced with the sweet smell of cakes and cookies, combined with the warm scent of fresh bread. Poppy was decorating a seven-tiered chocolate wedding cake with lemon frosting and delicate spun sugar flowers. With RASCH's money woes, she was baking less for the school and more for clients in the city.

"Need any help?" Olive hoped she did. Staying busy kept her mind off her failures.

Poppy motioned to the dozens of cupcakes waiting to be iced and decorated. "Maybe you can assist Auntie Winnie."

Olive nodded. Reaching for an apron, she heard, "Hello, ladies!"

Brood's frame darkened the open door. A weed trimmer was hoisted over his shoulder. As he entered, Brood seemed unaware that he was trailing dirt all over the bakery floor. "Something sure smells good in here!"

Poppy whispered to Olive, "He's been stopping by a lot lately. I think Brood's sweet on someone, and it's not me."

Auntie Winnie lit up when she saw the handyman. Shyly, she handed him a red velvet cupcake with a generous swipe of cream cheese frosting. When he took a bite, he broke into a shy smile.

"Winnie, you're the best," Brood said, bowing to her.

Olive allowed herself a tiny smile. Even if she was miserable and had no friends, it was nice to see other people happy.

31.
SWEPT AWAY

By the time Olive bid farewell to Poppy and Auntie Winnie, the sun had begun to set. She made her way to the DONUT TRESPASS! sign, trailing a hand along the chain-link fence. When Olive reached the area where the Misfits had captured the actors pretending to be pirates pretending to be criminals, she found the yellow crime scene tape broken and fluttering in the wind.

Olive stopped at the spot where she'd brought James down with her Snooze Vapors. Then she sat under the tree where Iggy had used the Time-Out String to tie up one of the fake crooks. The sky was turning gray, signaling a storm on its way, and the ocean began to ripple. Olive's heart grew heavy as she watched the water churn.

This was where the Misfits had come together in their biggest moment—and ultimately broken apart.

The wind whipped up the leaves like butterflies in a hurry,

almost making Olive wish she had a kite. Mimi used to have a fierce red dragon one that flew so high it looked like it was eating the clouds. In the distance, boats were bobbing in the water—water that was becoming darker by the minute.

Olive rose to return to Foggy Manor before the gray clouds split open. That's when she saw . . . *something,* right there, in the shallow banks being lapped by the waves.

Edging over to the shoreline, Olive looked down. Was it a box of some kind? She couldn't get close enough to tell, and to retrieve it would mean she'd have to get her feet wet. Olive cringed, kicked off her shoes, gingerly stepped into the ice-cold water, and reached toward it.

The first wave wasn't big, but it was strong enough to knock Olive over and push her under. Submerged and in shock, Olive felt her nerves snap awake. She struggled to stand as her feet touched the sandy bottom of the ocean floor. Her head was barely above water.

Instinctively, Olive chomped three times. "Help!" was all she had time to say as a second, stronger wave swept her out toward the sea.

The water churned nonstop as Olive gasped, fighting to keep from going under waves. *Is this how I'm going to die?* she thought as she flailed her arms, coughing up the salty water.

Panic kept pushing her down. Olive could feel her arms tiring. It was freezing. If only she had paid more attention during the Splish-Splash Splore!

Splore . . . *splore* . . .

What had Modest and Monica taught first and foremost? *Do not panic.*

Roll with the punches.

"Pace yourself," she could hear Monica telling her. "Most people lose a battle because they're tired."

". . . think of swimming like acrobatics under the water," Zeke had said.

Do not panic.

"Go with the flow," she could hear Mimi saying.

Olive forced herself to stop thrashing. She did the pendulum step in the water—back and forth, back and forth, one of the basics Monica had shown them in boxing. With her arms, Olive went from third position to fourth, like Modest had taught them—"Arms out!" he'd say. Third to fourth, repeat. Third to fourth, repeat.

"Arms out!" her grandmother would call up when Olive was on the tightrope. "It's all about balance."

Olive kept her arms in second position. She wasn't swimming . . . but she wasn't drowning, either.

Slowly, Olive found herself treading water.

By now, the sky was dark and the ocean was angry. She was a little way off from the shore and being pushed farther away with every minute. Olive could still see the island. The question was, How could she make it back? In the distance, Olive spotted BoBu returning to Foggy Island.

"Yash!" Olive yelled. But her cries were drowned out by the waves.

Then, to make matters worse, it started raining.

She closed her eyes. Olive was exhausted. She missed her parents, and Mimi. What were Modest and Monica doing right now? And the Misfits? She'd give anything to see them again.

"Ahoy, you there! Nice day for a swim?"

Great. Now she was hearing things. Olive struggled to open her eyes and saw a giant flamingo in the distance. Okay,

now she *knew* she was hallucinating. She wanted to go to sleep. Olive didn't know how much longer she could tread water.

Was she dreaming or was the flamingo getting closer . . . and was it being towed by Theo in a rowboat filled with Misfits?!

"Olive!" Phil's voice was as choppy as the waves, but it sounded like the sweetest music Olive had ever heard. "We're here!"

In an instant, fatigue was replaced with a rush of adrenaline, like the times Olive was on the trapeze, trusting Mimi to catch her. Only instead of her grandmother, the other Misfits were there, and Olive knew they weren't going to let her down.

"We've got you!" Iggy yelled from the boat.

"I'll save you!" James cried as he dove into the ocean.

Olive wasn't sure what was happening, yet before she knew it, the rowboat was close enough for Theo and Phil to drag her onboard. She was shivering, coughing up water, and colder than she'd ever been in her life—but she also had never felt happier.

After they wrapped Olive in a thick blanket, Theo and Phil managed to pull Iggy and James out of the water as well. Taking turns, they all rowed back to shore as the rain slowed to a light drizzle. Olive's heart lifted even higher when she saw two familiar figures waiting for them on the dock.

"Olive!" There was no hiding the worry in Modest's voice. "Are you okay?"

"Aren't you going to ask about me?" James was

shivering as they climbed out of the rowboat. "I jumped in the water to save her!"

Monica wrapped him so tight in a blanket that he looked like a mummy.

"What about me?" Iggy asked. "I jumped into the water to save you."

"I didn't need saving," James huffed.

"Well, you almost drowned the flamingo. . . ."

Theo shook the water out of his hair like a wet dog, spraying them. "You guys, just stop."

Phil scooched up next to Olive as the two best friends watched the others bicker. "Well, I'd say that the Misfits are back together."

"Yeah," Olive agreed, her teeth chattering noisily. "I was j-just p-pretending to be in d-danger to unite us," she joked.

"Maybe next time just call a meeting?" Phil suggested as the Misfits, overjoyed to be together, bickered and bantered, closing in around Olive to make sure she was really okay.

Warmed by their love and concern, Olive felt tears beginning to flow. At least she was already soaking wet, so no one could tell she was crying.

Modest looked like he was crying, too. "Darn rain," he muttered.

"Why are we all standing here?" Monica demanded. "It's freezing out. Everyone, inside for hot chocolate and cookies!"

Soggy but happy, the Misfits headed to Foggy Manor with their arms flung around each other.

32.
TREASURE CHEST

Olive wasn't the only one who hadn't given up wearing their ComChom and EarBuzz. Her call for help was heard by every Misfit. Theo had been aboard BoBu and had immediately insisted that Yash turn the boat bus around, citing the storm. Phil had tracked Olive flailing in the San Francisco Bay. Iggy had bolted out of her room, and James had thrown aside his book to join her. By then, Modest and Monica had been on their way, too.

That evening, the friends sat together in the dining hall for the first time in a week. It was Lasagna Night, but Poppy's garlic cheddar cheese biscuits were the highlight of the meal. Well, that and the Misfits' reunion.

"I missed you guys," Olive confessed. Phil reached over and squeezed her hand.

Iggy didn't even attempt to hide her smile. She bit into her biscuit. "Not me, didn't miss you at all." Turning to James, she added, "Are you crying?"

His eyes were wide open and full of water. "No! If I don't blink, the water is retained in my eye, and therefore the overflow doesn't run down my face and constitute crying."

"This means the Misfits are back together, right?" Theo looked hopeful.

All at once, they yelled, "Yes! Oof! Oof! Oof!"

Thinking they were instigating the RASCH cheer, the rest of the students in the dining hall joined in, and a cascade of *"Oof! Oof! Oof!"* showered down upon the Misfits as Primrose, Enid, and Ethel made sour faces.

Olive was so thrilled to be with her friends that it hadn't occurred to her to tell them *why* she'd fallen into the water in the first place. It wasn't until they were returning to their rooms after dinner that she remembered the image under the waves.

Intrigued, Phil stopped walking. "What *was* it?"

"I don't really know," Olive admitted sheepishly. "Probably nothing. It looked like a chest or container maybe?"

James perked up. "A treasure chest? That would be ironic, given the gala's pirate theme."

Iggy shook her head. "What are we waiting for? Let's go see what it is!"

Olive led her friends out of Foggy Manor and into the cool evening air, past a group of drama students who were pantomiming furiously, acting as if they were trapped in an invisible box. Even though it was night, Brood was trimming the rosebushes. The rain had stopped, and the scent of flowers and a salty ocean breeze whirled around them as the group neared the DONUT TRESPASS! sign.

James made sure no one was around, then signaled for them to turn on their flashlights. In earnest, the Misfits began to search the area around the fence for whatever Olive had seen. They split up, shining lights up and down the bank, but they couldn't find anything of interest.

After almost an hour, the Misfits were ready to give up. Olive was glad it was dark so they couldn't see her embarrassment. They had risked their own lives rescuing her from being washed out to sea—all because of something she'd only thought she saw?

"I'm sorry," Olive said into her ComChom. "Maybe we should just go back to Foggy Manor now and—"

"I found something!" Phil shouted into their EarBuzzes.

Closer to the shore, half-buried in the sand, was what looked like a small black suitcase. It took both Theo and Phil to pull it out of the shallow water.

"Could it be the Royal Rumpus?" Theo asked in a hushed voice. Olive had been thinking the very same thing.

Phil nodded, her eyes bright. "Probably stashed in there for the thieves to retrieve later."

Iggy reached for her tools and began to pick the lock.

"Security did a full sweep of the island before and after the gala," James noted as he rubbed his arms to warm them. "But not the water. This wouldn't have shown up on a metal detector or another land surveillance device—" He stopped midsentence when the lock clicked.

Slowly, Iggy lifted the lid. . . .

Disappointment swept through the Misfits. The black waterproof case was empty.

"Looks pretty fancy." Using one of her rings, Phil knelt to photograph it.

Iggy ran her fingers along the inside. "Bone-dry. It's lined with velvet and has a large cushioned compartment, three smaller ones, and a little one—shaped like a cat."

"The jewels . . . ," James started to say.

Heart pounding, Olive finished his sentence. "The stolen jewels were supposed to go in here. There was even a spot for Winky!"

"Clearly, the Bling King knew ahead of time which jewels to target," Theo deduced.

"The thief was going to hide the jewels," Iggy continued, "then smuggle them out later when the heat was off. . . ."

"But when we caught the decoy thieves near the water," Phil added, "the Bling King couldn't get to the case to stash them."

James gasped sharply. "What if security missed it, and the Royal Rumpus and other jewels are still on the island!"

A realization hit Olive like a bolt of lightning. "If we find the Royal Rumpus, we can save RASCH!"

The next morning, Police Chief Ruby Lopez strolled purposefully around the Laundry Room, picking up items—vases, books, an art deco lamp—and examining them.

"I like your theory," she told the Misfits. "It would certainly explain why we haven't recouped the jewels yet." She held up an empty bag of sour cream and onion potato chips. "Any more of these around?"

Theo fetched her a bag of chips. "Mind if I keep this?" Ruby asked. When he shook his head, she smashed it with her fist. "I like my chips small," she explained, before tipping the bag into her mouth. "Listen, I've got a source that says something's happening in the city. A big event that may or may not have anything to do with the Bling King. Plus one of the stolen jewels may have been spotted at a pawn shop in the Haight district."

She crunched on the chips thoughtfully. "That doesn't mean your theory is incorrect. Could be there was a second jewelry case that was picked up. Either way, we have to follow all leads. I can't send any of my people." Ruby tossed her empty bag into a trash can, then sat in James's banker's chair. Finding it uncomfortable, she switched to Iggy's recliner. "Don't want to scare off the bad guys. You kids up for checking it out?"

Olive felt her heart flutter as they nodded in unison.

"We can send them into the city on the pretext of a field trip." Reflexively, Monica tossed Ruby another bag of chips. "One of the other pods is going to the Karbon Art Museum tomorrow. They can take BoBu into the city with them."

The Misfits could not conceal their excitement. They were back in the game!

33.
LIZARD'S TAIL

After lunch, Olive tagged along with Theo to Butter Bakery. They took the long way so they could watch the whales off the far side of the island, and there was a spring in Olive's step that had been missing for a week. When they neared the bakery, the warm scent of sugary spices and pastries drew them in.

"Tarts!" Olive gasped, looking around.

Auntie Winnie pointed to the golden pastry with fluted edges cooling on the bakery rack. "I'm in charge of the jam." She puffed up with pride.

What the elderly woman lacked in baking skills, she made up with in eagerness. She offered Olive a boysenberry tart. It had just the right amount of sweet and slightly sour jam, and Olive noted that the confectioners' sugar glaze made it look like a priceless jewel.

Poppy emerged from the storage room, dabbing her eyes with her apron. Her face was red and bloated.

"Do you want me to take anything to the outreach center tomorrow?" Theo offered. He had devoured his apricot tart in two bites, while Olive was still nibbling on hers to savor it.

"Thank you, Theo—" Poppy began to sob. "But my sister is sick and I'm *totally* gutted. I need to fly home to London to be with her. I'm afraid I'll have to close the bakery until I get back."

Auntie Winnie stopped mashing blueberries. "Close the bakery?"

"Can't bake from London now, can I?" Poppy said in a failed attempt to sound lighthearted.

Olive remembered the time her mother returned from a business trip with a broken arm, and her dad had a broken leg. "Car crash," they explained. Olive was overcome with helplessness. She hoped Poppy's sister would feel better soon.

"I can bake," Auntie Winnie offered. When Poppy hesitated, she pleaded, "Let me try. Please, I know I can do this! Give me a chance."

"I'm not sure that's a great idea," Poppy was saying.

"We'll leave you two alone," Theo said kindly, and they exited the bakery. Besides, it was about time for them to head to the Laundry Room. There was something the Misfits needed to do.

Painful as it was, the afternoon was spent reviewing what went wrong with their first real assignment.

"I believe that, by now, you have all learned the importance of teamwork," Monica said at the end of their session. She paused for dramatic effect. "Not only must you work *together*, but you must also trust that your teammates won't let you down. We couldn't give you another mission until you learned this for yourselves."

"We learn from our mistakes and come back stronger," Modest told them. "Like the unlucky lizard who loses its tail from a cat attack. It flops around unsteadily, like it's dying. Then it starts to run around, and eventually, the tail grows back."

Upon hearing this, Phil and Olive glanced at each other and grimaced.

"We are constantly improving!" Monica reminded the group. "Phil, will you update your teammates, please?"

Phil approached the front of the room to unveil her newest accessories, including her Boomerang Bang, capable of toppling anything that weighed up to three hundred pounds before returning to the thrower. Most important, though, she had big plans for Vana, her self-driving van.

"No offense," Phil told Modest, "but we can't have you accidentally cutting off our communications again. That's why I propose that going forward, I have full access to the faculty lounge in person and remotely. Plus permission to create a Command Central in Vana for when we're in the field."

Monica's face was expressionless. Modest looked conflicted.

"Of course, you two would still be monitoring us from the faculty lounge," Phil quickly promised. "But this way we have one main point of contact—me—and we're covered in case there are any more computer or communication . . . incidents."

Not even Modest and Monica could argue with that, and suddenly Phil became in charge of Command Central.

By the next morning, the Misfits had formulated their game plan. According to Ruby's sources, there were rumors on the street that Winky, the stolen bejeweled cat, had been spotted for sale in San Francisco—though the sources hadn't yet figured out where. Upon arriving at the dock in the city with pod 38, Iggy and Theo would slip away to investigate the pawn shops on the north side of the Haight district. James and Olive would scour the south side. Phil would oversee Command Central from inside Vana while reporting to Modest and Monica.

They shared the ride on BoBu with the RASCH art pod, an undisciplined bunch. Olive couldn't imagine them to be NOCK, although she admitted the same could probably be said about the Misfits. Once Yash docked at the pier, the other pod romped down the plank, waving their arms and yelling, not even noticing that the Misfits were heading in the opposite direction.

As the group walked around the city, they couldn't help but notice how it had changed in just the past couple of weeks. When they passed a string of jewelry shops, they found them

shuttered and dark, with gates pulled over the windows and doors. Lost-cat flyers, used car ads, and KittyKon posters were plastered over boarded-up buildings. The Misfits stopped to stare at the headline in a newspaper box: "STERLING VANDERWISP OWES MORE MILLIONS—SOURCES CITE GAMBLING."

"Do you think Sterling could be the Bling King?" Iggy wondered out loud.

"I doubt it," James said. "Sterling doesn't seem like he has the brains to engineer a huge heist."

The Misfits made their way to the hidden alley, where Phil summoned Vana. Inside, they took a few moments to appreciate Command Central. On one of the screens, Monica and Modest were waving from their faculty lounge. "Look at me not touching any of the technology!" Modest held both hands in the air, then began to lean on the console, with his elbow headed straight toward a big red button that was labeled EMERGENCY.

"Stop!" the Misfits shouted. Startled, Modest jumped aside just in time.

Disaster averted, Phil pointed to another screen, showcasing Winky, the three necklaces, and the Royal Rumpus. "Ruby just sent photos of the stolen jewelry. I'll forward them to you for reference, but everyone should memorize what they look like as well."

Olive pulled her smartphone from her fanny pack and unfolded it. Phil's photos had already come through. Upon seeing them, Olive felt emboldened. Here was another chance for her and *all* the Misfits to prove themselves.

"Remember, if you come across the jewelry, *do not* confiscate it," Modest warned. He took a long sip of chocolate milk through a loopy straw. "Your job is to collect information, not stolen goods."

"Copy that," the Misfits said in unison, then commenced their official mission.

34.
BENNY'S PAWN SHOP

Three hours and countless shops later, Olive and James were no closer to finding the jewelry.

"Who knew there were so many pawn shops in San Francisco?" James grumbled.

"Come on, we only have three more left." Olive tried to sound upbeat, even though she had grown tired of his complaints over an hour ago.

They approached Benny's Pawn Shop, and when Olive pushed open the door, a bell rang. Inside, it was dark and dusty and smelled like a grandma's closet. A beautiful butterscotch-colored cat with blue eyes meowed from atop a bookcase. Old toasters, rusted bicycles, and a giant wooden bear crowded the room. On the counter were piles of broken watches, and inside a glass case was jewelry so old that the silver had turned dark gray.

She was about to leave, when James called, "Olive, over here!"

When she joined him, Olive couldn't believe what she saw. "Cats!" she said, gasping at the case full of cat-shaped items.

A young woman with a tall beehive hairdo emerged from the back room. Despite the NO SMOKING sign, she had a cigarette in her mouth. She scooped up the cat, who squirmed, trying to get away.

"It's a candy cigarette," she said defensively, even though no one asked. "I'm trying to quit. Don't judge me. Now, are you kids here to buy, sell, or steal?"

Olive tried to remember what Theo had taught them about making small talk to gain people's trust. She put on a warm smile. "We're just browsing. You have some very nice things here."

"Blah blah," the woman said, turning around with the cat. "My name's Jinx. Yell if you need me."

They waited until they could hear Jinx knocking things over in the office, then hurried to the glass display case crammed with cat mugs, cat salt and pepper shakers . . . and cat jewelry. There, among a tangle of cheap necklaces, was a black cat brooch with dazzling green eyes.

They had found Winky!

The two Misfits stepped out of the shop and into the sunlight, then burst into a little jig worthy of Modest, silently screaming for joy. Then, calmly, they re-entered the dark of Benny's Pawn Shop to photograph the evidence. Only by the time they got back to the display case, something was amiss.

In the minute they'd been outside, the case had been ransacked, and Winky was gone. *Again.*

Olive felt like she had been punched in the gut, but there was no time to dawdle. James checked behind the store while Olive tiptoed into the office and began to unzip her fanny pack.

"Hello?" Olive retrieved her Boomerang Bang, gripping it so tightly that her hands started to sweat. Their instructions were not to confiscate the jewelry—but they weren't supposed to let it be stolen (again), either.

The office was a cluttered mess with no Jinx in sight. Instead, a pounding was coming from inside a battered gray school locker.

"Jinx? Are you okay?" Olive was pushing aside piles of junk to get to the locker when James rushed in.

"Jinx jumped into a car and drove away!" he said, trying to catch his breath.

"What?! Then who's in there?" Olive pointed to the locker. The pounding was getting louder and more frantic.

James held his Time-Out String in front of him as Olive lifted the latch and yanked the door open.

Inside was a large man with his hands and legs tied up, a piece of duct tape over his mouth.

"Ah," James said as they helped him out from the locker and untied him. "You must be Benny."

As soon as the man's hands were free, he ripped the tape off. "*Ouch!* Yes, *I'm* Benny, and this is *my* shop! I paid some ditzy lady a hundred and eighty dollars cash for that cat pin! Then she has the nerve to come back, shove me in a locker, tape my mouth shut, and what? Steal it back? What kind of poopy scam is that?!"

James nudged Olive and snickered. "He said 'poopy.'"

Olive scowled. Into her ComChom, so only James could hear, she said, "Focus, James! We need to alert the others that we let the crook escape with Winky!"

In a flash, they left Benny and rushed outside. James chomped down three times to update the team.

"James here. Winky was sighted at Benny's Pawn Shop in our side of the Haight district."

When he paused, Olive chimed in. "Suspect apparently sold Winky to Benny and then . . . stole it back? She called herself Jinx, and she got away in a car."

"You let her get away?!" Olive winced at Iggy's outburst.

"Did you see what the car looked like?" Phil asked.

"It was small and brown?" James guessed. "No other details. She was too far away for me to see much."

"Copy that," Phil noted. "Stay put. Vana and I are headed to you."

Olive slumped against the side of Benny's Pawn Shop and stared glumly at the lost-cat flyers plastered top to bottom on a nearby lamppost. San Francisco sure had a lot of missing cats.

The fate of RASCH was in their hands, and she and James had let Jinx get away with Winky! How could they have been so careless? Olive couldn't imagine facing the other Misfits. She glanced over at James, who looked equally dejected as he sat on the stoop. He reminded her of a little kid in time-out.

Wait . . . that's it!

Jinx had shoved Benny into a locker and tied him up, but she'd left Olive and James alone because . . . they were just kids. She must have underestimated them, never considering that Olive and James would come after her.

Olive straightened her shoulders as Vana pulled up to the curb. She helped James up. "It's okay," she told him. "This game's not over yet!"

35.
JINX

By the time Olive and James climbed into the van, the rest of the team was already up to speed on the Jinx situation.

"If only we knew where she was headed," Theo said. They were all crowded around Phil, who was studying her various computer screens.

"Tracking Jinx now," Phil said without looking up. She had tapped into the security camera outside Benny's Pawn Shop and was rewinding through its records at quintuple speed.

"Stop!" Olive cried, pointing at the screen. "It's Jinx!"

Sure enough, the camera had captured Jinx jogging on the sidewalk with the cat, followed by James running out looking for her. Like a concert pianist's, Phil's fingers flew as she began accessing security footage from nearby businesses, until she tracked Jinx getting into a rusted old car.

"I can't get a good angle on the license plate." Phil sounded frustrated as she manipulated a shot of the vehicle on multiple screens at once. "Wait, are you seeing this?" She homed in on the sharpest image and then cleaned it up, enhancing the definition and getting rid of the shadows.

"Cats! It's not just the one she was carrying—Jinx is in a car full of cats," Iggy exclaimed excitedly.

"*That's* Jinx?" Theo squinted to get a better look. "I know her! She works at the Community Outreach Center. Jinx is the one I've been handing the pastries to."

"Oh no!" James said, sounding shocked. "*That's* how the jewels got off the island. Poppy must be mixed up in the jewel heist."

"Poppy?" Olive's eyes opened wide when it hit her. "I'll bet Winky was baked into the pastries!"

Iggy jumped in. "It's probably no coincidence that Poppy went to visit her 'sister' after Winky showed up in San Francisco."

Olive's stomach lurched. Poppy, baker extraordinaire, a master jewel thief? She didn't want it to be true, yet nothing else made sense.

Theo covered his face with his hands. "I'm the one who handed the pastries and gems off to Jinx," he cried. "I probably smuggled the Royal Rumpus off Foggy Island. I'm such an idiot!"

James patted him on the shoulder. "Been nice knowing you, pal. Why don't you make it easy for everyone and just turn yourself in now?"

"Theo," Phil consoled him. "There's no way you could have known. We'll find Jinx and get to the bottom of this!"

"Phil is right," Monica said through their Ear-

Buzzes. Olive had almost forgotten that Modest and Monica were monitoring them. Phil toggled the screens until she landed on Bee's camera in the Laundry Room, where Modest, Monica, and Police Chief Ruby Lopez were waiting.

"Modest. Monica. Ruby. What are our next steps?" Iggy asked solemnly.

Ruby tossed an empty bag of potato chips in the trash can. "The force has been updating me from the field. Combined with your new intel, we may explore a new direction." She leaned into Bee so that her face took up a full screen. "The Bling King is a jewel thief mastermind. This caper has a lotta layers."

"Layers? Like an onion?" Phil asked.

Ruby tapped her nose. "Copy that! James and Olive were able to interact with and identify a person of interest who goes by the name Jinx. Good job, kiddos! This is the first solid break we've had on this case, and if we play our cards right, Jinx can lead us to the Bling King."

Olive and James puffed up slightly. Suddenly they weren't the ones who'd let Jinx escape. Instead, they had identified a possible Bling King accomplice. Ruby continued, "We can assume that Jinx is a member of the Bling King Ring, albeit a rogue one. One theory is that Jinx pocketed Winky and was selling the brooch for a fraction of what it was worth. But why? That one-of-a-kind pin is valued at over a million dollars."

Olive started coughing like a hairball was caught in her throat. They had come so close to helping recover a million-dollar cat brooch!

"Maybe she didn't know its worth?" Phil suggested.

"Or maybe she did and was sending some sort of message to the Bling King?" Iggy ventured.

Theo was deep in thought. "Wait. So if Winky made it off Foggy Island, can we assume the Royal Rumpus and other jewels did, too?"

"Affirmative," Ruby confirmed. "However, these trinkets are so hot that no one can get them out of the city. Anyone leaving by plane, train, bus, or car gets searched."

"What about helicopter?" James asked.

"That too."

"Boat? Submarine?" James wanted to know.

"Those, yes," Ruby said.

"Bike? Kite?" James went on.

Ruby's jaw tensed. "Listen, kid. Trust me. NOCK's elite JAGS is on it. Our Jewelry and Gem Smugglers team is scrutinizing transportation of valuables, rather than the thefts."

"Let's focus," Monica jumped in. Through Bee's camera, the Misfits watched her pull a screen down from the ceiling of the Laundry Room. Using a laser pointer, she drew a line that went from Butter Bakery, over the bay, to the Bay Area Community Outreach Center. "We believe this is the route the gems took. However, the empty case was found here." Monica pointed to the DONUT TRESPASS! area. "Now I need theories starting with the waterproof jewelry case! Brainstorm! Let's go!"

James began. "Plan A—stash them there for later. But when we chased the decoy robbers and breached the no-trespassing zone, we brought security, and that plan was thwarted."

Olive winced as she relived the scene, then chimed in. "Plan B was to bake them into the pastries. Poppy must have had this backup plan in the works for a while—"

Theo picked up the trail, sounding slightly defensive. "Because she had an innocent, unsuspecting person who thought he was doing a good deed deliver them to a robber."

Phil patted his shoulder. "No one is blaming you."

"I kinda am," Iggy said.

"Could Poppy have stolen the jewels if she was baking for the event?" Olive floated the question. "Remember, the police cleared her the night of the robbery. Auntie Winnie was her alibi, and Brood confirmed that he stopped by the bakery the night she was there."

Mid-pirouette, Modest nodded. "Security footage places Poppy in Butter Bakery when the smoke bombs went off."

"Maybe she was merely an accomplice," Phil suggested. "Someone paid to stash the gems."

Iggy added, "A member of the Bling King Ring, maybe?"

James agreed. "When the heat got too hot in the bakery, she made a run for it." He grinned at his metaphor.

Modest stopped twirling. "So where is the Royal Rumpus now?"

Monica circled Benny's Pawn Shop on the map. "The mystery seems to have moved from Foggy Island and migrated to the city."

"Then that's where you'll find the Misfits," Olive announced.

36.
CLUES

At night, sleep eluded Olive. Thoughts of Dame Gloria, the Bling King, Jinx, RASCH, the Misfits . . . they were all jumbling together, around and around like laundry in the dryer.

As time had passed, Olive had grown to love Foggy Island, Foggy Manor, and especially her cozy dorm room. Phil and Theo had helped her put up strings of colorful pom-poms that reminded Olive of Mimi's circus tent. And on one of their visits to the city, after a round of hot fudge sundaes, the Misfits had crammed into a photo booth and taken goofy group pictures. Olive had framed hers, and she kept it on her desk.

To Olive, the Misfits were like their own version of *Meggie & Her Fun Family,* only with kid NOCK operatives.

With no sign of the Royal Rumpus, there was now less than a week before Dame Gloria was going to make good on her threat. And if that wasn't bad enough, she held a press conference offering a million-dollar reward for the Royal Rumpus, plus $250,000 for Winky, no questions asked. This threw the jewel heist back into the top of the news cycle again, putting even more pressure on the Misfits.

The formerly relentlessly cheery Sunny had turned into a walking storm cloud of despair. RASCHers, who used to flock to their dean, now hid when they saw her slumping their way. Even Modest and Monica took off running when she was near.

Gloom was cast over the school. The singers couldn't hit the high notes, the artists were having trouble mixing their colors, and film students kept forgetting to recharge their cameras.

NOCK hadn't come up with any new leads, and time was running out faster than the sand in Yash's hourglass. The Misfits had ventured into San Francisco several times, searching for Jinx and clues about the Bling King, but all they had come away with was frustration, KittyKon flyers, and a new respect for how fast Vana could maneuver around the city.

Back on the island, with nowhere else to go, Iggy and Olive headed to Butter Bakery to look for clues yet again. As they neared the tidy brick building, they saw that the light was on and the door was open.

"Auntie Winnie?" Olive called excitedly. "Is that you?"

"She isn't here," a gravelly voice answered. Olive and Iggy were startled to find Brood standing behind the counter, holding a bouquet of flowers and looking lost.

"The bakery is closed, didn't you hear?" Iggy said gently. "Poppy's . . . caring for her sick sister, and Auntie Winnie tried to keep the bakery open, but at Sunny's suggestion, she ended up taking some time off, too."

Brood shook his head and seemed surprised to find the flowers in his hand. "That's too bad." He shuffled past them and exited Butter Bakery. They waited until they were sure Brood was gone, then began to search.

Neither was sure of what they were looking for, but if Poppy was involved, then the bakery was still their only shot at clues. Maybe there was something the police had missed? NOCK had deemed the Misfits' theories top secret and not to be shared, lest a mole tip off the Bling King.

Auntie Winnie had left the kitchen a mess. Flour was spilled all over

the baking tables. Pans were piled in the sink, and batter had hardened in the mixer, resembling concrete. Lemon peels were piled up. Olive was sifting through large bags of sugar when Iggy shouted, "I think I found something!"

Jammed at the side of the oven was a *Fancy Cat* magazine. In addition to glowing articles featuring KittyKon, there were dozens of ads for elaborately decorated cat carriers, cat wranglers, cat portraits . . . You name it, it was there.

"Cats again," Olive was quick to note.

Iggy stopped at an ad that showed a cat wearing an over-the-top KittyKon crown and matching collar. "This is a bit much, don't you think?"

"There's something about the cats that is tying every-thing together," Olive mused, remembering all the flyers. "Between Winky, and Jinx's car full of cats, and now Poppy's magazine . . ." She gestured to the *Fancy Cat* issue. "Plus, with

KittyKon coming up . . . I don't know. Aside from the jewels themselves, doesn't it just *feel* like there's this big cat connection? Maybe the Bling King is planning something around KittyKon, especially since he seems to love publicity?"

"Olive, you might be onto something!" Iggy tucked the magazine into her fanny pack for safekeeping.

"Evidence does point to a feline connection," Olive surmised. "The lost-cat flyers could just be a coincidence, but there's an easy way to find out."

Yash steered BoBu out of the water and parallel parked in a tight spot on the street. "Darn kids," she complained bitterly, though Olive thought she saw a sliver of a smile. "What am I, a chauffeur?"

The Misfits watched her march off into the city to who knew where. Yash was very secretive about what she did on her trips—but then, so were they.

As the Misfits walked toward the area where Olive had spotted all the lost-cat flyers, they came across a two-story-tall screen outside the huge convention center.

"Whoa! Will you look at that?" Theo pointed up.

Fast-paced music (punctuated with meows) blanketed the street as a montage played, featuring all sorts of exotic cats, house cats, scruffy cats, and pampered cats. Footage of cats in fancy carriers danced across the screen, followed by images of cats wearing crowns. *"What time is it this*

Saturday? IT'S KITTYKON TIME!" a voice purred over the loudspeaker.

With the KittyKon music still ringing in their ears, the Misfits turned the corner to find the whole area plastered with lost-cat flyers.

"There are more of these now than before." Olive pulled a bunch of flyers down and started passing them around. "I've got a strong hunch that cats have something to do with the jewel heist."

Monica said to go with the facts, but Modest always countered that intuition and feelings were equally important. And Olive was confident about her suspicions.

"Cat burglar!" Iggy said, half-joking, half-serious.

She and Olive touched their noses and pointed at each other. Then Olive took out her phone and punched in the number on her first flyer.

"Hello," she said, sweetly. "I saw your lost-cat flyer—no, I'm afraid I haven't found your cat, but I was wondering if I could ask some questions?"

Following her lead, the other Misfits began making calls, too. Soon they found they were all receiving similar answers about the missing cats.

"Our cat went missing just last week. . . ."

"On Tuesday . . ."

"Expensive . . ."

"She was a show cat. . . ."

After, the Misfits huddled over hot fudge sundaes at Ghirardelli Square and discussed their findings.

"Why would all the cats disappear around the same time?" Phil asked as everyone handed James the cherries from atop their sundaes. "That can't be coincidence."

"It's got to have something to do with Jinx and Winky and the car full of cats," Theo said, digging into his sundae. "She always acted a little odd. Whenever I handed her the pastries, she'd just take them and toss the bag in a corner."

"Every time?" Olive admired the perfect balance of hot fudge and vanilla ice cream.

"A couple of times she grabbed the bag and disappeared into another room," Theo recalled. "It was always on lemon cake days."

James had a mouthful of cherries, but that didn't stop him from talking. "I'll bet lemon cake was a signal that the jewels were in the pastries!"

"That makes total sense," Iggy agreed. "Great thinking, James!" Everyone stopped eating and stared at her. "What?" she protested. "I can be nice now and then."

"Hold on!" Phil interrupted. "If Jinx sold Winky to Benny, pocketed the cash, and then stole the cat brooch back, maybe she did it more than once."

The Misfits let this settle in. Jinx could be the key to this mystery.

By the end of the afternoon, the Misfits had made over a dozen calls and created a list of as many lost cats as they could. From there, they went back to the pawn shops to check out Phil's theory. Several other pawn shop owners confirmed that it was Jinx who had sold them Winky and that she had stolen it back shortly after. None of them had reported it to the police.

"In my line of work, we sometimes deal in things that may or may not have been obtained legally, if you get my drift," one chatty pawn shop owner admitted.

They even returned to Benny's Pawn Shop to see if Benny had anything else to share, but he didn't have much to say other than: "She locked me in a locker. Who does that? Hey, kid, interested in buying a watch?"

As they headed to another pawn shop on foot, Iggy began to walk faster. "Everyone, pick up your speed!" she ordered in a low voice.

"Why?" James sounded annoyed. "You're not the boss of me."

Iggy activated her ComChom. "Don't turn around, but we're being followed."

37.
THE DECOY

The Misfits had trained for this. Wordlessly, they sped up, then split up. One year ago, Olive couldn't run around the block without getting lost. Now she was racing around the streets of San Francisco, eyes wide and focused.

"No one's following me," Olive reported into her Com-Chom. She slowed to a walk, careful to take note of her surroundings and the people nearby.

"Same," said Phil.

"Same," said Theo.

"Same," said Iggy.

There was a long pause, then James checked in. His voice was shaky. "I'm being followed. Bearded white man, reddish hair, average build, dark green corduroy shirt, and jeans. I'll lead him to the alley by the gas station on Geary Boulevard."

"We'll meet you there," Phil said, and Olive started running again.

She was the first to arrive and was surprised to find James chatting calmly with the bearded man. Still, Olive stayed in the shadows and gripped her Boomerang Bang, just in case, as she crept a little closer.

"You scared me!" James was laughing with the man. He didn't look like he was in danger, but Olive noted that James might be acting. He was surprisingly good at that.

"So sorry! I didn't mean to scare you," the bearded man apologized. As soon as he spoke, Olive realized he was one of the fake thieves from the gala. "I just recognized you from that night," he said to James. "Hey, what's that perfume you just sprayed me with? It stinks!"

James looked surprised to find that he was holding the Stink Spray. As he slipped it into his pocket, Olive relayed to the others, "James appears to be safe. But stand back. He's talking to a decoy thief from the gala."

"So strange that you fell asleep in the middle of the biggest jewel heist of the century," the bearded man said, not unkindly. "Do you have narcolepsy? You know, that thing where people can fall asleep anywhere?"

James tugged on his bow tie. "I just get bored easily."

"Did you see me on TV?" The man reached for his phone and played a news clip. "I was interrogated by the police for three hours before they realized I was innocent. I'm kind of a celebrity now." He puffed up his chest.

"Really!" James sounded impressed. "What was it like talking to the police?"

Olive smiled. James was leading the conversation toward the Royal Rumpus.

"They wanted every little detail. Only I was so nervous I forgot to tell them all sorts of stuff!"

"Like what?"

"Like that the person on the phone who hired me said to stay away from the water. But then I messed up and ran toward it, so I didn't get paid!" The man shook his head. "If you know anyone who wants to hire an unemployed actor, I'm Rance Reed, performer extraordinaire!"

The Misfits regrouped at a picnic table in the Presidio, a former army base turned national park. Tourists were milling about as they began brainstorming. Iggy passed around the bag of oversized hot pretzels Theo had bought from a street vendor.

"Remember," Phil said, squeezing a packet of mustard on hers, "this is Blue Sky, meaning there's no limit to how outrageous an idea can be. The only rule is that we can't make fun of anything someone says."

Everyone looked at Iggy, who rolled her eyes.

"I'll start," James volunteered, waving his pretzel in the air. "The last time there was a jewel heist as big as the Royal Rumpus was over fifty years ago. A necklace called the Empress Immortal was stolen during a fancy dinner party. Like the Royal Rumpus heist, other jewels were taken at the same time, and most of them were eventually recovered. But the Empress Immortal was never found." He paused, eyes lighting up. "The jewel thief's nickname was the Cat."

"The Cat?!" Olive stopped chewing. "We know that cats are somehow involved in *this* heist. But why? Is he sending a message, maybe?"

Theo jumped in. "Maybe the Bling King is a relative of the Cat? His son, maybe? Or grandson? Maybe it's Jinx!"

James shook his head. "Trust me, it's not Jinx. She's way too scattered."

"Cats, cats, cats." Phil wiped some mustard off her face with a napkin. "Let's set the heist aside for a moment and focus on how the jewels will be smuggled out of the city."

"Oof! The cats are carrying them!" Iggy shouted.

"You might be onto something," Olive was quick to agree. "Show them the *Fancy Cat* magazine," she said to Iggy, who removed it from her fanny pack. Olive pointed at the cover. "Look at what all these cats are wearing. What if the gems are smuggled out on cat collars? There would be so many fake jewels, the real ones would just blend in."

"Ruby said that they're searching all forms of transportation." Phil was pacing now. "But she didn't say anything about pets being searched!"

Iggy nodded excitedly. "All the missing cats had to have been stolen, and they were all expensive cats and show cats. The kinds of cats that would be at KittyKon."

Theo chimed in. "It's like, if Phil can hide microphones in retainers, a jeweler could easily plant real gems next to fake ones on cat collars."

By now all the Misfits were walking in quick circles. From a distance, it probably looked like they were square-dancing.

Olive was getting dizzy, so she started walking in the other direction. "The airport will be overrun with cats when KittyKon is over," she said. "The Royal Rumpus and the other jewels can be transported out in plain sight."

"How can we know which cats have the jewels on them?" James wondered. "There will be hundreds of them. Too many to count."

"I can create an app to identify the missing cats," Phil assured them. "All you'd have to do is hold up your phone like you're taking a picture. The app will scan the room and ping if one of the missing cats is identified." She took off one of her rings and held it up. "And this is my GemDetect. It's programmed to glow when near authentic gems larger than ten carats, within a twelve-foot radius. This can help signal when we're close to something extra valuable—"

"Like jewels from the Royal Rumpus," James and Theo said in unison, then high-fived.

The emerald ring. It looked like a smaller version of one of Phil's computer rings. "Whoever wears this needs to be super stealthy," she noted.

Iggy raised her hand.

"Since they'll be our primary eyes and ears, it'd also help if they were nimble and even-tempered," Phil continued.

Iggy put her hand down, and everyone looked at Olive.

38.
KITTYKON

"I have my doubts," Ruby confessed. The Misfits stood at attention as everyone gathered in the Laundry Room. "Monica, Modest, what do you think about the Misfits' theory?"

Monica went first. "The facts tell us that something odd about cats is happening in the city. Coincidentally, it's at the same time the Bling King wants to unload the Royal Rumpus and other jewels, and Winky was spotted in several pawn shops. But it is very far-fetched."

Modest flexed his biceps and did a couple of squats to loosen up. Then he posed perfectly still with his fingertips on his temple. At last, he patted his belly. "My gut tells me that the Misfits are onto something big, and that we should trust them."

Monica nodded slowly. "I agree. Here are some more facts. These kids were selected because of their unique points of view and stellar skills. I know this is unprecedented, but

231

when we assembled this team, we all knew it wasn't going to be business as usual. Cats are an outlandish assumption, but then so is a group of undercover operatives their age."

Ruby rubbed her neck. "I think I've heard all I need to know," she said. Olive's heart sank until the police chief continued. "Okay, Misfits, you're good to go. Security and local law enforcement will be on alert as backup, but we'll keep the full story within NOCK. If it checks out, then it's all on you kids to bring us home."

The Misfits joined Modest in a cheer before getting serious about their assignment.

"I give us a ninety-two out of one hundred chance," Iggy told the others.

"Ninety-two percent chance that we'll be successful?" Olive asked hopefully.

Iggy shook her head. "Ninety-two percent chance that we'll fail. Anyone who wants out, speak now."

The room went silent. Olive had never seen her friends look so determined. They were too close to the finish line now and as ready as they were ever going to be.

When Vana pulled up in front of KittyKon at the convention center, Olive could swear the building seemed bigger than the other day. Had it grown? Had they shrunk? She didn't feel like an elite crime fighter trained by world-class NOCK operatives. She felt like a nerdy middle school kid who was in over their head.

No one moved or made a sound. No one looked like themselves, either. Everyone except Phil, who was at the helm of Command Central in Vana, was wearing disguises. Since the thieves had been at the gala, the Misfits couldn't risk being recognized.

Olive's wig was long and curly, and she wore a private school uniform. Theo had a short blond wig and a collared shirt. Iggy was wearing a checkered dress and pigtails, and James was in overalls and a San Francisco Giants baseball cap.

Olive checked her fanny pack and accessories for the umpteenth time. "What are we waiting for?" Phil asked impatiently.

Taking one last deep, calming breath as the van's sliding door opened, Olive shouted, "Okay, Misfits. Let's do this!"

Inside KittyKon, it seemed like every cat wore a bejeweled collar. Many of the people did, too, and hundreds were dressed in cat costumes. As the others went in search of Jinx and lost cats, Olive kept casually waving the GemDetect ring, waiting for it to glow green. Finding a diamond among millions of rhinestones seemed impossible.

All at once, her nose began to tingle and she started getting a strange feeling. Slowly, it grew, until—

"Achoo!" Olive let out a giant sneeze, startling herself and everyone around her. Then she sneezed again, and again. She sneezed so many times that people clutched their cats close and backed away.

Olive was suddenly reminded of why her parents never let her have a cat. She was allergic to them! So much for being stealthy!

"Achoo!"

Olive fumbled through her fanny pack. It was full of life-saving accessories, but nary a tissue. Her nose was running and her eyes were watering.

A woman carrying a basket of kittens tapped Olive on the shoulder. "Hun," she drawled in a sugary southern accent, "you should try KittyKat Alley. They sell allergy relief remedies."

Olive *achoo*ed past the endless booths selling this and that until she saw it . . . SNEEZE-B-GONE, HERBAL CAT ALLERGY RELIEF. The salesman wore a top hat that Olive could just make out through her watery eyes. He gave her a sympathetic smile as she paid for the medicine.

"These will do the trick," the salesman promised. A curious orange tabby peered over the top of his hat as Olive popped a tablet into her mouth. "You might get sleepy at first, but then you'll be fine!"

He wasn't wrong. While Olive's sneezes started to let up, she also found herself growing extremely drowsy. She stumbled in the crowded aisles, blinking sleepily, and when she was mid-yawn, her ring began to glow green! "Something's near aisle twelve," she reported into her ComChom. "My ring is lighting up."

"Olive, I'm close by," James jumped in. "I've identified a lost cat with my app."

The two met up and, with James's direction, tailed the catnapper toward a booth that sold cat collars. But by the time she reached the end of the aisle, Olive was having a lot of trouble keeping her eyes open. Maybe just a little nap would help. . . .

She woke to James flicking water on her face. Olive sat up and rubbed her eyes. "What happened?"

"You fell asleep in the middle of our mission," he said wryly. "Guess I'm not the only one to—"

Phil's voice roared into their EarBuzzes. "Stop goofing around! I've got eyes on all of you via the security cameras. Jinx is with the catnappers at the Creative Cat Collars booth. The lost cats are fitted with bejeweled collars that can only be removed with special tools. I need GemDetect confirmation *stat.*"

Adrenaline chased away Olive's sleepiness. When she neared the booth, she saw that Theo was already there. Her ring began to glow green again.

"Say cheese for *Meow Majesty* magazine!" Theo quipped, taking photos of a cat being outfitted at the booth while James slipped a tracker, thin as a thread, around the cat's paw. Nearby, as Olive scanned the crowd, watching her ring—

"Pimple!" Iggy's voice came over their EarBuzzes. "Repeat. Pimple! Pimple!"

"Misfits, pay attention!" Phil's voice was calm but forceful. "James and Olive, Iggy has a Code Pimple and needs your help. Theo, stay on the mission. Track the cats! Find Jinx!"

With Phil guiding them, Olive and James pushed through the crowds, amid a chorus of *"Hey!"* and *"Where are your manners?"* and *"Meow!"* At last, they spotted Iggy, who was cornered against a booth by a tall woman and a huge man. Both were wearing sunglasses.

"Why are you following us?" the man demanded.

"I'm trying to find my dad. You look like him." Iggy tugged on one of her pigtails and started crying. "He's ugly, too."

"She's just some stupid lost kid," the woman said, sounding bored.

Olive immediately recognized them from the gala. The mirrored sunglasses, the tailored black suits, the snooty attitudes . . . they were Dame Gloria's elite bodyguards!

"One of *them* could be the Bling King," Olive observed.

"More likely part of the Bling King Ring," Phil replied over her EarBuzz. "I'll bet they weren't working for Dame Gloria—they were working for the jewel thief! He probably pays better than she does."

"You're coming with me," the man growled, reaching for Iggy's arm.

"Not gonna do that," she said sweetly. Then Iggy crouched and executed a spinning sideswipe kick, knocking him over. Before either bodyguard could react, James grabbed a cat and rubbed it in Olive's face.

"What are you doing?!" cried both Olive and the cat's owner.

"Distract!" James ordered, just as Olive's nose began itching.

"ACHOO!" On cue, Olive started sneezing violently, ramming right into the bodyguards, bouncing off them like a pinball. When they glared at her, she stuck a finger in her nose.

"Achoo! Sorry! *Achoo!"*

Confused and disgusted, the bodyguards backed away, giving Iggy a chance to escape. Immediately, the bodyguards were in pursuit, joined by two more. "Keep them away from the Creative Cat Collars booth," Phil instructed.

"Copy that!" Iggy said gleefully.

Dodging the crowds, Olive and James headed to the booth. When they finally arrived, a butterscotch-colored Himalayan cat with blue eyes was being fitted for a collar.

Olive squinted at the cat—it looked so familiar. Her Gem-Detect ring began to glow.

"The Aphrodite Diamond!" Phil said in a hushed voice.

Sure enough, when Olive got a closer look, the priceless jewel was the centerpiece of the cat's new collar. Just as James reached for the cat's paw—

Out of nowhere, Jinx emerged from the back of the booth, scooped up the Aphrodite cat, and held it close. "Step away!" she said sharply to James. "This one comes with me."

"Photo?" Theo said, cheerfully snapping away. "I'm from *Meow Majesty* magazine."

"No photos!" Jinx growled—giving James just enough time to slip past and place a tracker on the cat's paw.

39.
AIRPORT

"Got it, let's go!"

Phil had confirmed the tracking on the cat with the Aphrodite Diamond, and the Misfits dashed outside to join her in Vana. They quickly buckled themselves in, and as the van eased into traffic—

"What?" Iggy scowled at James. "Stop staring at me."

James laughed. "You look so weird with pigtails," he said.

"Well, you don't look so great in overalls, Mr. Farmer," Iggy huffed. "Hey! Want to see something cool? I managed to swipe this from that bodyguard who's so full of himself!"

"A pen?" James was unimpressed.

"It's not just any pen," Iggy said, awestruck. "*This* is military grade, with a tactical laser that can cut through metal and glass." She gazed at it the way Olive looked at Poppy's caramel butter shortbread squares. "I've always wanted one of these."

As Vana maneuvered through traffic, Phil kept track of the Aphrodite cat. "It appears we're headed to the airport," she informed the others. "According to the security cameras outside the convention center and the trackers on some of the felines, it's not just the Aphrodite cat we're trailing—there's a caravan of others in carriers headed there."

"Makes sense," Theo agreed. "My Lost Cat app went into overdrive the minute I neared the Creative Cat Collars booth."

James stopped trying to pull Iggy's pigtails as she laughed and swatted his hand away. "Airport?" he said. "Looks like the Royal Rumpus and the rest of the jewels are going on a trip."

"Not if we can stop them," Iggy declared.

Vana's shortcuts took them off and on the freeway, through side streets and alleyways, until they finally pulled up to the airport.

"Look!" Theo pointed. "There's even an Express Kitty-Kon security checkpoint." He leaned over Phil, who was watching via the airport's cameras.

"They're taking the cats out of the carriers," Olive observed. "The carriers are searched, and so are the people . . . but pets aren't even given a second look."

"Then, that'll be our job," Iggy said, straightening. The Misfits exited the van while Phil reported to Monica and Modest.

Once they'd successfully slipped past airport check-in thanks to a clever trick from Phil at Command Central, she instructed, "Head to the Captain's Club. I spotted Jinx heading inside. Plus people carrying cat carriers are lining up to enter, too.

"Theo, charm your way into the room, then open the emergency exit for the other Misfits to enter." Phil paused. "Everyone, be careful."

The Misfits, still in disguise, walked quickly through the airport, following signs to the Captain's Club. Hidden, Olive, James, and Iggy watched as Theo approached the lady at the front desk. She was wearing a necklace made of macaroni shells.

"Greetings and meow," she greeted Theo. "Name, please? You have to be on the list to be let in."

"I'm Mac . . . um, Caroni?" He pointed to her necklace. "Family heirloom?"

She brought her hand to the pasta strung on a shoelace. "My son made this when he was in kindergarten."

"I made one for my mom, too."

"What a nice boy you are," the lady said, smiling fondly. "Go right on in, Mac."

Knowing Theo was safely inside, the Misfits snuck down an employees-only corridor and waited for Theo to let them in. When the emergency exit door to the Captain's Club opened, they slipped in unseen.

Soon Olive was in position, crouched behind a garbage can, watching Jinx count cats. Dame Gloria's bodyguards stood by her side, arms crossed. Two more bodyguards joined them, holding what looked like special bolt cutters.

"The Bling King Ring," Olive breathlessly reported to Phil.

"Hurry up and get in line!" Jinx yelled. The cat carriers had been emptied, and the catnappers were holding the lost felines. Jinx bent toward one cat, plucked a familiar-looking brooch from its collar, and pinned it to her jacket.

Olive nudged Theo. "Winky," she whispered, motioning to Jinx.

"On your mark, get set," Iggy whispered over their Ear-Buzzes, *"GO!"*

The Misfits barreled toward the Bling King Ring, spraying them with Stink Spray.

"What?!" hollered a bodyguard, who was removing a collar. The cat she was holding took one sniff, then fought successfully to get away. More cats followed suit, repulsed by the spray.

"Get the little brats!" another bodyguard yelled upon seeing the Misfits.

"Hold on to your cats!" Jinx screamed over the confusion.

"Your special delivery has arrived," Phil said calmly into Olive's EarBuzz. "It's at the back door."

Ducking under a hard punch aimed at her head, Olive raced to the door to greet their secret weapon: actor Rance Reed, the former faux pirate. Today he was dressed as a dogcatcher.

"Who let the dogs out?" he sang loudly, wheeling in two huge gift-wrapped boxes. "Woof! Woof!"

Olive popped the lids off the boxes, laughing with delight as dozens of canines scrambled over each other to escape. Dogs raced toward the shocked catnappers and cats. Shouts of panic, confusion, woofs, and meows ricocheted around the room.

"Priorities!" Jinx screamed at the crooks. "Get the *cats,* not the kids!"

Just then, the front desk lady swung the lounge entrance door wide open. "Everything all right in there?"

In an instant, cats and canines charged out the door and into the open airport, followed by Jinx, bodyguards, and Misfits.

"Backup requested," Phil broadcast. "Special Unit Police Force and Humane Society volunteers are on their way."

"Closing in on a bodyguard," James reported. With their ComChoms on override, the Misfits could hear a *THWACK!* and *OUCH!* followed by James's "Gotcha!"

Olive turned her focus to Jinx, who had a tight grip on the Aphrodite cat. As the two ran through the airport, no one gave them a second glance. People were always running to catch planes. Jinx stopped to bark at a dog who was chasing her, and when she did, the cat escaped from her arms.

Quickly, Jinx went after the feline, with Olive closing in on her. Jinx picked up speed as she rounded the corner toward the far end of the airport. Olive did a flying leap over a chair, then was startled to a stop. Sterling Vanderwisp was relaxing in an empty passenger terminal, trying to pet the Aphrodite cat, who wanted nothing to do with him!

Olive's mind was racing a mile a minute. Was Dame Gloria's grandson the Bling King?! Sterling was at the airport . . . then there were his gambling debts, which were all over the news . . . then the smoke from his show . . . not to mention his questions regarding Royal Rumpus insurance money . . .

Olive knew she needed to proceed with caution so as not to alert Sterling or scare the cat away. "Pimple! Pimple! Sterling Vanderwisp is in on the heist!" she broadcast

over her ComChom. "I've got my eyes on the Aphrodite cat, and Jinx is somewhere near, too!"

Still unsure of who the Bling King was and who was part of the Bling King Ring, Olive could feel that she was about to find out. But just then, she heard a familiar voice.

"Hello and pecan puff pastries!" Auntie Winnie sang as she waltzed toward her in a flouncy floral dress.

Olive didn't realize she could be more shocked than she already was. "Auntie Winnie?!" she sputtered.

"Hello, ladies!"

Olive swiveled around. It was . . . Brood, and he was holding a bouquet of flowers!

"Auntie Winnie!" Gallantly, he bowed. "I thought I'd find you here."

"Sunny suggested I take a vacation, so I'm treating my-self to a little getaway." Auntie Winnie fluttered her eyelashes at him. "Brood, you rascal. You've been after me for a long time."

"True, that." Brood winked back.

Just then, Jinx appeared, clutching the catnapped cat. Olive realized where she had seen the cat before—it was in Benny's Pawn Shop. Her ring began to glow green.

"There you are!" Jinx shouted above the barking. By now, several overly enthusiastic dogs had joined them.

Sterling Vanderwisp pointed to himself. "Me?"

In a smooth, swift move, Brood tossed the flowers up in the air. When they exploded into a shower of colored smoke, Jinx froze. In that second, Brood grabbed the cat from her arms and took off running.

He can run? Olive was shocked. What happened to his limp? Wait! Could Brood be the Bling King?!

"What's happening?" Wobbling, Auntie Winnie clutched her heart as Olive chased after Brood. "I'm so confused."

By now, Jinx had tackled Brood, and the Aphrodite cat was on the loose again. Sterling pulled out his camera and began filming as dogs slobbered all over him. "Everywhere Sterling Vanderwisp goes, fans fight over him," he intoned, immediately posting it for his InstaFriends followers.

Olive reached for her Slinky. Unsure of which one of them was the Bling King, she did a swift circle glide around Brood, Jinx, and Sterling, then tugged tight on the wire.

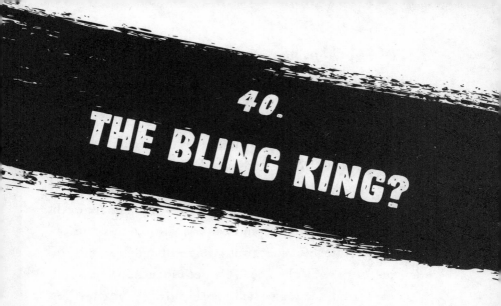

40.
THE BLING KING?

Iggy skidded around the corner, followed closely by Theo and James. They braced themselves when they saw the trio all tied up and yelling at each other.

"The rest of the Bling King Ring bodyguards are entangled with Time-Out String." Iggy paused to catch her breath. "But where's the Aphrodite cat?"

"I think Brood might be the Bling King," Olive said, gripping her Boomerang Bang in one hand and her Snooze Vapors in the other. She bent over and removed Winky from Jinx's jacket. "I'll take that." Olive pinned it to her own shirt for safekeeping.

"You meddling kids," Jinx spat. "My grandma's not going to like this!"

"Your grandma?" Olive asked, surprised.

"Let me go," Brood insisted. "I can explain."

"Let *me* go," Sterling ordered. "Or else I'll tell *my* grandma on you!"

James tapped Olive on the shoulder. "Um, is that Auntie Winnie?" He pointed out the window of the airport terminal. Sure enough, Auntie Winnie was outside, sprinting across a runway with her dress hiked up . . . and carrying the Aphrodite cat.

"Attention, Misfits." It was Phil. "All flights have been halted due to the canine and cat overrun. I locked in on Auntie Winnie headed toward some abandoned airport hangars, but I've lost her. Sending Bee for backup."

"We'll find her," Iggy said confidently. She reached for her tactical laser pen and cut through the bolt on a door that led to the tarmac.

As trained, the Misfits split up, each taking north, west, east, or south. After looking high and low, Olive was about to crawl under the belly of a plane when it started: a tickle in her nose, followed by her own violent sneeze. *"Achoo!"*

She startled. This could mean only one thing: the allergy tabs had worn off—and there was a cat nearby.

Olive's eyes began to water. She put on her FoggyGogs to stop from rubbing them, then attached the nose clamp to cut down on the sneezing. Auntie Winnie and the Aphrodite cat were close, she was sure of that.

In the distance, Jinx and Brood were together—or was one chasing the other? They must have gotten out of the Slinky. Either way, James was in hot pursuit, followed by Theo.

A squeaky wheel alerted Olive to an airport employee pushing a baggage cart nearby. The urge to sneeze was huge, especially after she heard a meow. Olive peered around an airplane tire and spotted Auntie Winnie wearing the orange baggage handler vest. Instead of luggage, the Aphrodite cat was in the cart, and they were headed toward a helicopter.

"Stop!" Olive ordered, gripping her Boomerang Bang.

Auntie Winnie faced her and smiled, freezing Olive in her tracks. The elderly woman had an evil glint in her eye, and Olive almost didn't recognize her. She held the cat up high.

"Drop your weapon, my dear. You hurt me, I hurt the cat."

Olive slowly did as she was told, holding her hands up. Her GemDetect ring was glowing. "Auntie Winnie." There was a tremor in her voice. "It was you? You've been working for the Bling King all along?"

Auntie Winnie's laugh was so cold that Olive shivered. "That is so sexist. There never was a Bling *King*. Everyone assumed a man took the Royal Rumpus." She smirked. "Let me introduce myself. I'm . . . the Cat."

"The Cat?!" The Cat was one of the greatest thieves in modern history, Olive recalled. "But he retired decades ago!"

"*She*"—Auntie Winnie sounded bitter—"has never retired. I just never got caught—and I never will." As Auntie Winnie stroked the cat in her arms, the Aphrodite Diamond glistened in the sunlight. "Such ageism. Olive, my dear, please let the world know that the Cat is back, and better than ever. I'm tired of these new, young jewel thieves getting all the publicity."

The blades of the nearby helicopter began to whirl. Olive silently thanked Phil for her FoggyGogs as the wind picked up, hair whipping around her face.

"Oh! There's my ride." Auntie Winnie backed away. "It's been nice getting to know you, Olive Cobin Zang. Let me know if you ever want to come over to the other side. I could use someone smart like you." Her eyes fixed on Winky, still pinned to Olive's shirt. "Join me and I'll make sure you get a dozen Winkys!"

Auntie Winnie tossed a handful of Bling King calling cards in the air, and the wind from the helicopter blades carried several toward Olive. Snatching one as it flew by, Olive looked at the card and was slammed with a jolt of recognition. It wasn't a crown on the card after all. . . . It was a cat's paw!

Sweet old Auntie Winnie had played them all . . . but the game wasn't over yet! Olive was so close to saving RASCH, there was no way she was going to let this criminal slip away yet again.

Mimi's letter to her mother flashed in front of Olive. She could practically hear her grandmother saying, "If you believe in something, keep trying, and don't be afraid to fail."

Olive clenched her fists. She looked between the cat, Auntie Winnie, and the helicopter. Auntie Winnie was moving swiftly, but so was Olive. There were no doors on the helicopter, allowing the jewel thief to take an impressive flying leap and land squarely in the passenger seat.

"Go!" she growled at the pilot.

When it started to rise, Olive jumped, lunging at the metal skid bar at the bottom of the helicopter. She gripped it tight and could feel herself being lifted off the ground.

"*What* are you doing?!" It was Phil's voice. "Olive, let go before it's too late!"

Olive tightened her grip as the helicopter rose higher. Instead of feeling scared, she was filled with a familiar rush of adrenaline. It was exactly like holding the trapeze and flying through the air at Mimi's. Well, okay, maybe the helicopter could fly quite a bit higher and her grandmother wasn't there to catch her this time. But even as the chopper flew over the airport buildings, Olive could hear Mimi's reassuring voice telling her, "You are braver than you know."

"Stay calm, Olive. I'm sending in reinforcements," Phil's tone sounded reassuring. "Bee's nearby—that's how I can see you." A whoosh of relief embraced her when Olive spied the little drone flying alongside her.

Auntie Winnie leaned out of the helicopter, looking down at Olive. The helicopter blades chopped up her words, making it impossible to hear. Olive wasn't sure how much longer she could hold on.

"Do not panic," she reminded herself.

Olive began to kick her legs and swung back and forth, until she hooked her knees over the skid bar. Now she was hanging upside down like a sloth, which was a hundred times more comfortable than hanging from one arm.

Phil's calm voice came through. "It's just you and me right now, Olive. I've muted everyone else. Bee has a safety cable attached to her, and she can hold your weight easily. I want you to secure it to the loop on your fanny pack. Make triple sure it's on tight, okay?"

"Copy that." Olive reached her hand toward Bee.

Overhead, Auntie Winnie was yelling, but Olive still couldn't hear. The thief dangled the Aphrodite cat from the helicopter, gripping its collar tight, and appeared to be laughing. The terrified kitty clawed the air frantically as if trying to swim.

Still upside down and hanging by her legs, Olive began to swing back and forth confidently, as if she were on the trapeze getting ready for the biggest catch of her life. Gaining speed, she recalled Mimi's words of advice:

You need to trust yourself.

Olive took a deep breath, then swung up and held out her arms—only this time, instead of grabbing on to her grandmother, she snatched the cat from Auntie Winnie.

"Give me that cat!" Auntie Winnie screeched.

Holding the trembling feline tight, Olive knew this was her moment. In a steady voice, she broadcast into her ComChom, "We're headed home." Then she released her legs from the skid bar and began to fall.

There was a beat of silence, then Phil spoke again. "Olive, I've activated Bee's safety cable. You'll feel a hard jolt—that means it's working." At that, Olive felt a reassuring yank on the cable as Bee held her from above. She smiled. "Hold the cat tight," Phil continued. "Stay calm. We're here for you. I'm putting the others back on."

Olive was strangely at peace. There wasn't much she could do up here other than put her trust in Phil and Bee.

Iggy came on through her EarBuzz first. "It's Olive . . . and a cat flying in the sky!"

"You got this, Olive!" Theo reassured her.

"Hang on!" James cried.

From above, Olive looked at the Misfits, their heads tilted toward her. They were growing bigger as she came closer. All had their arms raised in the air, ready to catch her. Before Olive's feet even touched the ground, she got the best hug of her life as her friends crowded around, with the cat squirming and mewing in the middle.

Olive looked around at the tears on everyone's faces. It didn't matter to the Misfits that they were now in possession of a catnapped cat with a multimillion-dollar diamond on its collar. What mattered was that Olive was safe.

When Olive pulled off her FoggyGogs, she was surprised to find that she was crying, too. Just then, a familiar voice came on. "Olive, Misfits, excellent job. Meet at the airport security office."

"Thank you, Phil." Olive meant that with all her heart. "For everything. I can't wait to see you.

"Me too," her best friend answered. "Me too."

41.
HOME

The Misfits and the Aphrodite cat were whisked to the airport security office. Between all the cats, dogs, and catnappers, airport security seemed at a loss, while the police tried to sort everything out. Ruby was waiting with Phil, who ran up and embraced Olive.

"Thank you for saving my life," Olive said, trying not to cry again.

"Anytime," Phil promised. She smiled. "We did okay for a couple of dorks, didn't we?"

Ruby cleared the room of everyone but the Misfits. "The jewels and catnappers are accounted for, but it's still raining cats and dogs. Dame Gloria has been notified that the Royal Rumpus has been secured. It seems Sterling Vanderwisp actually did have a plane to catch this afternoon." She paused. "We'll still question him, and he may be called to testify against Auntie Winnie. The video he uploaded of himself captured her in the background absconding with the Aphrodite cat."

James nudged Iggy. "Told you he wasn't smart enough to be involved."

Ruby tapped her nose, then pointed at James. "Well done, Misfits. Bringing in dogs to separate the cats from the catnappers was brilliant."

Olive blushed. That had been her idea. She was glad James had thought to call Rance Reed for the job.

"We've got cat wranglers flying in to locate all the felines—after all, most are still wearing priceless collars," Ruby continued. "Olive, when you made your request for dogs, Monica immediately sourced the canines from a local Humane Society. Volunteers are on-site now rounding them up. TV crews are covering the chaos. The good news is that all this publicity will help the dogs find homes."

"We did it!" Iggy cheered, and the others joined in until Ruby cut the celebration short.

"I hate to tell you this, but unfortunately, the Cat managed to sneak out from under our radar."

"Auntie Winnie—I mean, the Cat escaped?!" Theo sounded stunned.

Olive looked thunderstruck. "I should have stopped her!"

"Listen up," Ruby said sternly. "Your job was to recover the jewels and the Royal Rumpus, and you did that swimmingly." She pointed to Olive's shirt. "Looks like you even got Winky. Revealing the identity of the jewel thief was icing on the cake."

That reminded Olive of someone. "Is Poppy going to prison for helping the Cat?"

The police chief shook her head. "Nope. She's been cleared. Poppy was duped by 'Auntie Winnie.' Seems that when the Cat first learned that the Royal Rumpus might make an appearance at the gala, she pretended to be a dotty old woman and talked her way into a job at Poppy's bakery weeks in advance. She's been planning this caper for a long time.

"Now, pay attention," Ruby ordered. "Remember, no one can know that any of you were involved with this. We're scrubbing the airport security cameras right now." She smiled wide. "Great job, you've represented NOCK well! You kids are amazing."

"She's right," James agreed. And with that, the Misfits let out a rousing "Oof! Oof! Oof!"

Once they were released, the trip to Foggy Island was strangely peaceful. James was exhausted. Phil was exhilarated. Theo's wig kept sliding off, and Iggy's pigtails were drooping. Olive had forgotten to remove her nose clamp. If Yash thought anything was odd, she didn't mention it.

There were two people waiting at the pier to welcome the Misfits home. Modest rushed forward, tears flowing. "I was so nervous," he blubbered, blowing his nose with such force that nearby seagulls stopped in midair. "Hug!"

As the Misfits folded Monica and Modest into the group, Olive's heart swelled. She couldn't believe that when she first got to Foggy Island, she couldn't wait to leave. Now, more than anything, she wanted to stay. Without a doubt, Olive knew she'd found where she truly belonged—here at RASCH, with the Misfits.

42.
CLUE

A couple of days later, a boisterous game of Clue was underway in the Laundry Room.

"It was Auntie Winnie in the bakery with the Royal Rumpus," Olive joked during James's turn.

Modest and Monica had ordered celebration pastries from Poppy after she returned, following her sister's successful gallbladder surgery. Phil selected a sugared snickerdoodle and a trio of mini macarons. As Iggy reached for a lemon tart with a delicate meringue tower, there was a heavy knock on the door.

"The cat wranglers got all the cats," Ruby reported, strolling purposely toward the pastries. "We got all the catnappers—and the collars."

"Did all the lost cats get reunited with their owners?" Theo wanted to know.

"All but one." Ruby bit into a chocolate chunk brownie

with a crusted caramel topping that was so delicious she was momentarily speechless. "No one has claimed the Himalayan that was wearing the Aphrodite Diamond yet. But speaking of cats, Jinx has been especially talkative. She's been complaining that her grandmother, the Cat, didn't give her enough allowance and that she was forced to sell and resell Winky for spending money."

Ruby helped herself to two more brownies, wrapping one in a napkin and slipping it into her pocket. "I've got someone waiting in the hallway who can fill you in on more."

A slender, older man in a stylish navy suit and dapper fedora strode confidently into the room.

Upon seeing him, James dropped his cookie onto the floor and Iggy choked on her tart.

Brood took off his hat. He had shaved his stubble and cut his hair close to his head, and looked completely different. "I'm one of you. NOCK, NOCK! I've been after the Cat for decades, but she always manages to elude me. This is the closest I've ever come to capturing her."

The Misfits stared at Brood, not believing their eyes.

"I wanted to thank all of you in person. In my years with NOCK, I've seen a lot of smart and brave operatives, but you kids rank among the top. I've even told Anonymous that."

"Do you report to Anonymous?" Phil asked.

"Not directly," Brood admitted. He gave Monica and Modest a friendly nod. "I work for the Mouse, the Cat's arch nemesis, who also reports to Anonymous. When we got a whiff that the Royal Rumpus might be targeted, the Mouse came out of retirement to help NOCK on this case. They sent me here, undercover."

Olive could not believe what she was hearing. The Mouse? The Cat? *Brood* was NOCK, too?

"The Mouse has been feeding us intel. They know the Cat better than anyone," Ruby said. "Dame Gloria is thrilled that she got the Royal Rumpus back, even if the jewels were separated. A master jeweler is almost done reconstructing the necklace, and she's planning to wear it to the premiere of her documentary, *Glorious Dame Gloria, Our Living Legend.*"

"Does this mean RASCH won't be shut down?" Olive asked hopefully. The others leaned in anxiously.

Ruby smiled broadly. "Yes . . . and not only that, but it also means that you kids get the million-dollar reward!" The Misfits all gasped in unison, and James fell out of his chair. "Congrats! Oh yeah, plus that additional $250,000 for the return of Winky."

For once, the Misfits were speechless.

43.
THE MOUSE

Ruby stayed to kickbox with Monica, but Brood had a plane to catch. Before he left, he tapped Olive on the shoulder. "Walk with me around Foggy Island for a bit, will you?"

The bay was sparkling and the sun was shining. They stopped to marvel at a humpback whale, rising out of the water in a breathtakingly high breach, as if showing off.

Brood pulled a white box with a yellow bow from his suit pocket. "I met with the Mouse yesterday. They asked me to deliver this to you personally."

"For me?" Olive's curiosity went into overdrive. She pulled on the ribbon, lifted the lid, and stared.

Inside was a familiar ceramic mouse writing a letter. As she ran her finger over the tiny chip on the mouse's ear, Olive's head and heart felt like they were about to burst.

"My—my—my . . . grandmother is the Mouse? Mimi is *alive*?!"

"I am not authorized to confirm that." Brood's eyes sparkled like he knew a secret. "I'm not going to deny it, either. The Mouse is tracking the Cat at this very moment. I'm sure they will be in touch with you soon." He dipped his head, smiling. "Farewell, Olive Cobin Zang. It's been a pleasure working with you."

Then, just like that, Brood was gone.

The sunlight blinded Olive momentarily. Still holding the ceramic mouse to her heart, she felt flooded with a million emotions. Her heart was beating so fast, she could barely breathe. Olive shut her eyes and tried to regain her balance, when she imagined she heard a familiar voice shouting in the distance.

"Olive!"

Her eyes fluttered open, and she did a double take when she saw her parents running up the path. "We're back!" her mother cried, embracing Olive in a tight hug.

"I'm here, too!" her father confirmed, pointing to himself.

Olive was dizzy with shock and joy. Dazed, she hugged her mother and told them excitedly, "Mimi's alive!"

"Technically, no one said she had died," her father replied.

Olive took in a sharp breath of air. *"You knew?!"*

"I know it's been hard on you," her mother said apologetically. "Your grandmother swore us to secrecy. If the Cat even got a whiff that Mimi had come out of retirement, her cover could have been blown and her life put in danger."

Olive stared at her parents. They knew about the Cat? They knew that Mimi was the Mouse?!

"I read your diary," her mother confessed. "How could I not? It was so intriguing! So dramatic. You have a flair!"

"We both read it," Dr. Zang Cobin admitted. "I'm going to try to be less boring. Maybe take up a hobby."

"Wait." Olive felt unsteady. "You aren't mad?"

"How could we be?" her mother replied. "You were being true to yourself, though"—she looked contrite—"we never knew we made you feel so alone. But we're here now."

"We've turned down our next business trip so that we can bring you home," her father said, looking pleased.

Olive's heart swelled. They had never passed up a business trip before. Still . . . "I didn't really mean all that stuff in the diary," she tried to explain. Near the dock, Modest, Monica, and the Misfits were running around, doing jetés and punching each other. As much as Olive wanted to see her parents, she longed to stay put with her friends.

Her father was still talking. "Maybe I could get that new lawn mower I've always wanted. I could teach you how to mow the grass!"

Her mother laughed. "Olive doesn't want to mow the lawn, but maybe when she gets back to her old school, she can run for student council or take up a sport."

"I appreciate that you're willing to skip your business trip," Olive quickly cut in. "But if I'm honest, I'd love to stay here, at RASCH—if that's okay with you."

Her parents looked at each other, smiled, and shrugged. "If that's what you want," her mother gamely agreed.

Olive broke into a wide grin. They were letting her stay! She waved cheerfully at Sunny, who was striding purposely toward them from across the lawn.

When the dean approached Olive's parents, she embraced them and said, "It's been too long!"

"Should we tell Olive?" her father asked her mother.

Tell me what? Olive wondered.

"She excelled at her assignment," Dr. Cobin Zang confirmed, looking proudly at their daughter. Sunny had a secretive smile on her face.

Olive was about to ask when her father said in a rush, "We're with NOCK, too!"

Olive was stunned. "*You're* No One Can Know? Both of you?!" She couldn't believe it. She couldn't even *begin* to believe it. It had never occurred to Olive that her parents might actually be interesting.

"NOCK is practically the family business," her mother said merrily. She plucked a feather off her lapel. "Your grandmother brought me in. It's where I met your father, and now you're in it, too!"

Dr. Zang Cobin handed her a snow globe. It was from KittyKon.

Olive glanced uneasily at Sunny, then motioned to her parents to stop talking about NOCK. But the dean didn't appear to be paying attention. Instead, she riffled through the pockets of her voluminous caftan. She found a bag of lemon drops and offered them around. "Your family's secret is safe with me," she assured Olive.

"It better be," her father said, laughing. He popped the sour candy into his mouth, puckered up, then discreetly spat it out.

Olive was confused. "You know about NOCK," she said to Sunny.

The dean winked. "You're good at word games and puzzles, right, Olive? Scrabble, Bananagrams . . ."

Olive nodded.

"Then what's my name?" Sunny asked.

"Sunny O'Moa," Olive told her.

"Is it?"

Olive shut her eyes and visualized the letters that spelled "Sunny O'Moa." As she moved them around in her head, everything became clear.

Sunny O'Moa . . . was Anonymous!

EPILOGUE

That night in the dining hall, Enid and Ethel kept pretending to yawn in the Misfits' direction, egging each other on. It was their idea of being clever, Olive assumed. Looking directly at the Misfits, Primrose said loudly, "They are *soooo* boring!"

"It's true!" James shouted, confusing her.

"I like being boring," Phil proclaimed. The Misfits laughed.

They were in the middle of figuring out how to spend their reward. After much discussion, it was decided that most of the money would go into a safety fund for RASCH, even though Dame Gloria had pledged to increase her donations to the school. A portion would go to the Bay Area Community Outreach Center, and a portion to the Humane Society. And a small amount would fund a Misfits' Hot Fudge Sundae Club and a group subscription to *Meggie & Her Fun Family.*

After dinner, they all headed to their rooms, except for

Olive. "See you in a bit," she told the others. "I'm going for a walk."

Outside, the crescent moon's glow cut through the darkness as Olive made her way up the familiar path toward the fence. In the distance, Foggy Manor was lit up, looking warm and inviting. As Olive neared the DONUT TRESPASS! area, she heard a rustling sound. She whirled around and bent down.

"I thought it was you." Olive slipped on her FoggyGogs and nose clamp and then picked up Queenie—the Himalayan cat who had worn the Aphrodite Diamond collar. When Sunny found out that the cat had gone unclaimed, she'd said, "It's about time Foggy Island had a mascot, don't you think? Yash, bring her home."

Olive gave the butterscotch cat a hug. They had been through so much together. "Do you want to visit the swans with me?"

Queenie purred contently, then startled at the sound of leaves crunching nearby. Olive whipped around, holding the cat protectively to her chest.

"Don't be scared, Olive," someone said.

Before she could activate her ComChom, Zeke stepped into the moonlight. He motioned for her to be quiet. "I'm in danger, and I need your help," he whispered. "They're after me, and I don't know who to turn to."

His normally confident demeanor had been replaced by fear. Olive nodded to Zeke. "I just happen to know some people who may be able to help you," she said.

Whatever threat he was under, Olive was sure the Misfits could take it on.

AGENT PROFILES

OLIVE COBIN ZANG
- Remarkably unremarkable
- Skilled acrobat
- Allergic to cats

PHILOMENA "PHIL" SAATCHI
- Tech specialist/inventor
- Wears her computers (what, you don't?)

JAMES HARMON
—Too passionate about Battleship
—Certified genius

IGNATIA "IGGY" AMARA INZAGHI
—Combat specialist
—Not really a "people person"

THEODORE "THEO" WINTHROP III
—The mellowest of the Misfits
—Friendly and good-natured, excellent at talking to grown-ups

GADGET PROFILES

MISFITS PHONE

Disguised as a regular phone, it stores several high-tech custom-created apps. It can be folded or rolled up if needed.

STINK SPRAY

Long-lasting fart-smelling spray that can be used on assailant to identify them later. Or use it on yourself to repel people.

ULTRA STICK

Sticky substance that can jam doors shut, glue shoes to the ground, and stop heavy machinery.

FOGGYGOGS

Allow you to see through smoke and fog. Can be used as swimming goggles.

BEE

Powerful tiny drone with super-stealth capabilities.

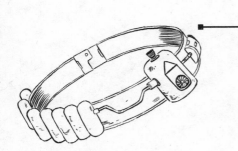

COMCHOM

aka the Communication Chomper. Looks like a dental retainer. Talk to your teammates by chomping down three times and speaking without opening your jaws. Can also be used to make your voice sound different.

ACKNOWLEDGMENTS

Just like the Misfits, who rely on each other as friends and colleagues, I have a whole slew of people who, whether they know it or not, helped me write this book.

A huge shout-out to my Northampton squad, Jarrett Krosoczka, Grace Lin, and Mike Curato, for your constant companionship and encouragement. Phil Baker, your witty texts keep me laughing. Mary Peterson and Wilson Swain, I love our Zoom-y talks. And Dan Santat, we were unpublished when we first met, and look at us now! Your wonderful illustrations brought the Misfits to life (plus this gives us even more excuses to have lunch together).

To the marvelous team at Random House Children's Books: without you there would be no Misfits Mysteries. Sincere thank-yous to Shana Corey, Caroline Abbey, Mallory Loehr, Michelle Nagler, Judith Haut, Barbara Marcus, Carol Ly, Jen Valero, Barbara Bakowski, Alison Kolani, Rebecca

Vitkus, Kris Kam, Dominique Cimina, Erica Stone, Katie Halata, Adrienne Waintraub, and John Adamo.

Tricia Lin, my amazing editor: your insights, encouragement, and love of a good twisty mystery have taken this book to the next level. Jodi Reamer, my (secret) agent: I can imagine you being a Misfit when you were a kid. Speaking of kids—to my son and daughter, Benny and Kait: your wild creativity and youthful antics are a constant inspiration. Mom and Dad, thank you for being there for me. And to Rob, whose belief in me has never wavered: this book is for you.

ABOUT THE AUTHOR

© Emi Fujii

LISA YEE has taken a private-investigator course, and it's slightly possible that she's a secret undercover operative. She's also a Newbery Honoree and a National Book Award finalist for *Maizy Chen's Last Chance.* Some of her other twenty-one novels are the groundbreaking *Millicent Min, Girl Genius; Stanford Wong Flunks Big-Time;* and the DC Super Hero Girls novel series. A frequent contributor to NPR's Books We Love, she divides her time between Western Massachusetts and Los Angeles.

LISAYEE.COM
@ @LisaYee1

ABOUT THE ILLUSTRATOR

DAN SANTAT is a #1 *New York Times* bestselling author and illustrator of over a hundred books. His picture book *The Adventures of Beekle: The Unimaginary Friend* received the Caldecott Medal. He also illustrated *The Blur, Lift,* and *Drawn Together,* all written by Minh Lê, which received critical acclaim. Dan is also the creator of the Disney animated hit *The Replacements.* He lives in Southern California with his family.

DANSANTATBOOKS.COM

@ @DSantat